LOW LIFE

Mike Duff

This novel was joint winner of the Crocus North West Novel Competition in 1999, judged by Livi Michael, Danny Peak and Karline Smith.

First published in 2000 by Crocus
Crocus books are published by Commonword Ltd,
Cheetwood House, 21 Newton Street, Manchester M1 1FZ.

Commonword gratefully acknowledges financial assistance from the Association of Greater Manchester Authorities, Manchester City Council and North West Arts Board.

Crocus Books are distributed by Turnaround Publisher Services Ltd, Unit 3, Olympia Trading Estate, Coburg Road, Wood Green, London N22 6TZ.
Cover photo by P-P Hartnett.
Cover design by Ian Bobb.
Printed by Seddon Printers, Unit 6 Kay Works, Moor Lane, Bolton BL1 4TH.

British Library Cataloguing-in-Publication Data. A catalogue record for this book is available from British Library.

To the best cornermen a man could have in the boxing match of life: Ted Taylor and Pete Thwaites; and to - the best years of my life spent in the arms of another man's wife - me Mam. Love and Peace, Duff.

LOW LIFE

It was the best of times, it was the worst of times. Like fuck it was. What did Dickens know about anything? We all knew Magwitch would end up being Estella's old man.

Anyway fuck that, what I'm gonna tell you about is Kiters, Moochers and Bagmen, and Funny Red Nose day in Bolton. Fucking Bagmen, easier living than Catholic priests.

Me right, I was working in this shitty job for the City Council. What I did was book all their vehicles into the garage for service, repair and M.O.T. and what have you.

Nice little earner; the driver would hand the keys over to me, I'd make him sign a form. Then I'm supposed to check the vehicle and pass the keys on to a Supervisor. Like fuck. I realise we're a man short, a link missing from the chain, so I introduce the Duck to the scene. They called the cunt that cos his name was Donald.

Now I'll tell you something about mechanics - the only thing lower than their I.Q.s is their sperm count. Listen, at the time, I was running a five-a-side game of football, we played once a week. The pitch cost twelve pound, there's twelve of us play, a pound a piece, dead simple. Yeah, I do a name card every Thursday as well, ten pound the winner and ten pound towards the football pitch. Like fuck - I got a bottle of vodka with it every Thursday for two years. Then one day this fucking labourer, not a fucking mechanic notice, says,

-Why'd you do a card? - we've already paid.

Net result - end of an earner.

Jug Ears they called the labourer, no prizes for guessing why; he was always boasting about three in a bed sex romps with him and his missus. Got me own back on the big mouthed bastard, his wife fucked off with another man. So I wait till the canteen's full and I shout over to him,

-Hey Jug Ears, these three in a bed romps you were telling me about - was that you, the missus and the twat that's tomming her now? Ha ha, no fucking answer to that !

Listen, I'm losing it a bit here; I started off about kiting cheques and I ain't even finished with the Duck yet. Right, I get the keys, I give them the Duck and he takes anything worth having out of the vans...copper, locks, materials, tools, whatever. He gives me the keys back, I check the vehicle out with a Supervisor, do a list of contents. No comebacks that way. Once a week we have a weigh in and once a week we flog parts, materials and tools to the Dog Shit man. Nice little earner. Until one day the City Council launch a secret enquiry which everyone including the cleaners knew about. It was thorough - it left no stone unturned. They came in the dead of the night; checked all lockers, interviewed everyone concerned. Then sacked this fat bastard for having guttering in his car - fucking wankers.

Anyway, that's the point me story begins; at the time I had a wife and three kids so I needed all the extra money I could steal.

A good kiting gang consists of five members - two Moochers, two Kiters and a Bagman. What a sensible Moocher does is work out of town. Manchester's been hammered. Cockneys think that they are the real wide boys, but the only ones with any real bottle are Mancunians and them sad bastards Scousers. Listen, I'll tell you how fucking clever them Cockneys are. We were down at Wembley one year and four of us queued up for beer. I orders eight lagers; this Cockney barmaid pours them, as she's pouring them I'm passing them over me shoulder. She passes me the eighth, asks for some ridiculous amount, enough for a deposit on a house in Collyhurst, and I say,

-and eight pasties as well please love!

She turns round to microwave the shite and we disappear behind a sea of faces. Typical Cockney. You try that at Old Trafford and some dyslexic ex-Rampton psychopath with MCFU typed on his knuckles recreates his lobotomy, with you getting the part that Bob Hoskins would get if it was a film.

My motto's always bin - 'When in London act like George Formby and rob the cunts blind' - a case of 'Turned out nice again, motherfucker'.

Anyway, point made.

The Moochers train it out of Manchester Victoria, which boasts a beautiful domed ceiling in the bar, or Manchester Piccadilly, which is good for sheep shagging land in Yorkshire and the Potteries.

Me brother-in-law Robbie, who's the Moocher in this story, worked alone as a sort of cost cutting exercise. Mainly because he couldn't find a partner of equal bottle, but most Moochers work in twos.

What they do is wear boiler suits or some other sort of work gear, walk past the security into large firms and attempt to get into empty offices, cabins or cloakrooms. Then go through the coats, bags, desks and what have you, one moocher keeping an eye out for the other. Once you make a hit you get out as soon as possible. If you're stopped along the way you just say

-can you direct me to Personnel? or,

-any jobs going mate?

You have a central rendezvous place, usually a pub or a cafe in case you get split up. If it comes on top it's women, children and drag artists first.

You concentrate on cash, cheque books and cheque cards; always take diaries, cos arseholes who work in offices rate brainwise between mechanics and Scousers and usually, believe it or not, write down their PIN number. One time Robbie got a card, book and diary from this shit hole of a firm in Batley. On the train home he goes through the diary for something to do. Fuck all of interest - the cunt ain't shagging the boss's wife or anything. Then at the back he comes across four fucking numbers. Now you don't have to be no Magnus Magnusson to figure out what they are. Robbie gets to Manchester, slings the card in the hole in the wall, and Bob's a strange man who your Aunty swears is her husband. The till gives him two hundred plus a statement saying there's another sixteen hundred available.

Anyway, Robbie hits a different till the next morning expecting the knock back, but the till gives him another two ton. The silly wanker in Batley hasn't noticed his gear's gone. No wonder their fucking Variety Club went broke. Over six days Robbie did the cunt for twelve hundred, then on the seventh day the machine did one with the card.

The poor fucker must've got a bank statement or something, or maybe just went in his coat pocket and found the stuff gone. Either way it was a pretty expensive fucking error.

Never keep anything on you, follow the golden rule of all crime - Get it, Stash it, Deny it. If all goes well you've made a good butty; enough for the wife, the ganja, the drink and the train fare tomorrow. If the Moocher has copped for any cheque books and cheque cards without pin numbers he has three choices. He sells them at the going rate, at the time £4 a cheque, get a book with twenty in and you're on an easy eighty quid. Second choice is kite the cheques yourself. Third is work with a couple of Kiters for a percentage.

The latter is the agreement me and Robbie had. I was the Kiter for the male books and his wife, Clarissa did the female ones. Robbie acted as our Bagman even though he had no need, as he had already done his bit.

A good Kiter spends as long as necessary on the signature until he's got it right in his own head. Don't believe all this shit about three days and all the cheque book names and numbers are on Stolen Lists. The Police only circulate to the area the books are stolen from. So, if your book is from Rotherham you can fly your kite all over Bury. Anyway if you think about it, to have all the stolen books on one list you'd need a list like a Rothmans Football Yearbook. Remember to do a barge pole on Manchester. You can't even cash your own cheques there without some fucker asking your mother's maiden name.

Fair sized towns are a good bet, even better if they've got a Debenhams, Lewis's, Chelsea Girl etc. Kite as many cheques as you feel sorted with. Every time you do one in, pass the gear to the Bagman. That way, anything goes wrong - and it fucking does - you're not left tear-arsing up Market Street carrying four Legos and a Babydoll nighty.

Don't let the Bagman accumulate too many bags. I knew a lad - Sellotape he was called - we called it him cos when he was about seven he had his glasses held together by Sellotape. So Sellotape sort of stuck to him forever! Everyone called it him; I didn't realise he didn't like it till years later we're sat in the Heywood Arms pub when this lad says to him,

-Get the beer in Sellotape.

Sellotape turns round punches him and says,

-You never went to Corpus Christi, don't fucking call me Sellotape!

Anyway, he was working as a Bagman for Kilkenny Benny, he had about eight bags of whatever with him that they'd kited someplace the day before. It's nine in the morning - I ask you, who the fuck has that sort of shopping at that sort of hour? What they were planning on doing was the swopsie as they went along - Benny kites one while Sellotape returns one.

Tough shit; this have-a-go hero Security Guard on three fucking pound an hour and a new uniform once a year decides to make a citizen's arrest. Sellotape loses it and commits the cardinal sin and butts the arsehole. Pandemonium breaks out and poor old Sellotape in the end is apprehended by four pensioners on a fucking outing.

Net result - two years.

So, like I say, too many bags ain't recommended.

Last man on the team is your Bagman. There are two sorts of Bagmen; one's your working sort who's also a Moocher or Kiter and the other sort is your leaching shit, like Scots John. To be a Bagman you need about as much bottle as Mussolini had when he attacked Abyssinia. Basically, you just mind the bags while the Kiter's doing the work, and if you're doing the swopsie you take the stuff back the next day. Simple enough; if you buy a coat, forty-eight quid in British Home Stores Burnley, you go back to British Home Stores Bolton the next day with your goods receipt and say,

-Sorry, unwanted present

and get a cash refund. It took the big stores years to catch onto that, and by that time as you'll see, I'd well and truly got me fucking come-uppance.

You'll gather I don't like Scots John. Well I don't - dirty bastard did a credit fraud walkout using my Dad's ID, the week after me Dad died. Honour among thieves? Like fuck there is. That cunt couldn't even hold on to an imaginary friend, let alone a fucking real one.

BUMPING

I'd better kick off with a bit of background information on the people concerned in the story; the majority of them are as bent as Brazilian free kicks. But I'll give you a sort of family tree of infamy, regardless.

My name is Ronald Rafferty, also known in the Sodom that is Central Manchester as Rooftop. I was born in Cheetham Hill twenty eight years before this story begins, so at the time I was roughly the same age as Jesus was when they gave him some practical experience of some fellow carpenter's work, and just as good a conman. Though I consider myself a Cheetham boy I spent most of me early life existing in a upstairs maisonette in a place called Miles Platting, which is a kind of open asylum for the Criminally Insane. Speaking of maisonettes, the wankers who decided to design a flat roof building for a city famous for rain want their arses kicking, and the toss-pots on the Council who passed the design, if they didn't get a good butty out of it, want a lot fucking worse.

Anyway me, I've had a pretty chequered career in both crime and what you might call more conventional employment. I once was forced to resign from a job at the Social for sending giros to meself. Good little earner that. I sat next to this girl called Becky, she was a grade below me and she wrote out the giros. One of me jobs was to check that she'd written them out right and post them. Well to cut a long story short I had a pocket full of envelopes with one or more of me accommodation addresses on. These were made out for Bumpers' addresses.

A mate of mine Big Tony used to sort out the Bumpers. What he'd do is gain entry into a Tower Block, wearing a boiler suit and a City Council donkey jacket, find an empty flat, force the door open and change the Yale lock. That way we had a safe address for any crime we fancied.

We called them Bumpers' addresses cos in the main that's what we used them for; ordering lots of furniture and electrical goods with fake ID and bumping the firms. Getting identification was piss simple - what you did was get hold of a wage slip, union card, old electric or gas bill, anything; join a library in that name and then open a bank account using the same. Nowadays that ain't so simple, but believe me three or four years ago you could walk into the Yorkshire Building Society in Piccadilly with just one form of ID, tell them you're starting work on the Monday and you want your salary paid direct into their account. I'm telling you, bung them a fiver and you could walk out of there with a passbook.

Next stop is hit the Town Hall and have a look at the Electoral Roll. You've got your three forms of identification, including a bank book so all you want now is a name that corresponds to the ID. Any area will do though it's usually better to choose somewhere fairly decent like Didsbury or Withington -sure to have a good credit rating there, don't want to pick some cunt who's blacklisted. Where possible also choose a date of birth you or one of the team can pass for. So now you're cooking with gas - you've got a name and address, say,

-A.Smith
14 Clegg Street
Withington.

and you've got a wage slip, a bank book and whatever else, union card, whatever. Then you hit the big stores; Laskys, BHS , whoever,

-Hello, I'm interested in a television and video recorder.

The smiley bastard salesman is seeing pound signs.

If necessary pay the 10% deposit. It doesn't really matter if you're getting the stuff to order, no harm in paying £150 down for £1,500 worth of gear if you've got some punter willing to pay you £600 on delivery.

I'll tell you, I've walked round Boardmans in the morning with a woman, had her point out which three piece suite she wanted, give me the deposit and I've been back in the afternoon and had some smart arse young kid snatch me hand off.

The tricky bits are the credit agreements:

-Name?

-A Smith

-Address?

-26 Albert Court, Miles Platting

-How long have you lived at that address?

-Five months.

-Are you on the Electoral Roll from there?

-Yeah, I think so; if not try my old address, 14 Clegg Street, Withington.

Sweet as a fucking nut. The cunt serving you is on 2% commission and a shit wage so he doesn't want the deal to go down on him any more than you want him to go down on your little sister.

-What day can we deliver?

-Monday, the wife's in all day.

Lots of firms will let you take the stuff with you. If not, no real problem. Get to the Tower Block, throw an old carpet in the hallway, put a bit of net across the door. Half paint the hall walls and sling down a couple of old dust sheets. Monday when the delivery van comes, you can watch its approach half a mile away.

-Drop it here mate, we're painting in the living room.

If everything goes right you've done four in a week then it's move on to a different address.

It's a bit of a shit trick on the randomly selected individual from Withington, a bit like the way God gives out cancer. Imagine the Direct Debit to Boardmans ain't honoured, so they start to send threatening letters to the Tower Block. They get no reply, so then they trace him back to his last known address and hound him for payment. Do a County Court judgement against him and he can't buy an Evening News on credit this side of Newcastle. Poor cunt's got a zero credit rating and his character is totally fucked by someone he don't even know.

Anyway back to the story - this girl, Becky used to pass me the giro, I put her envelope in me left hand pocket and took my envelope out of me right hand pocket. I always had the envelopes written by a third person so fuck all's in me own handwriting. I always zoomed in for the ones under £20 for two reasons - easier to cash, in those days post offices weren't stipulated and secondly, I didn't like to think of a family going without food. Anything under twenty was for a single person and the cunt should've been working anyway. All was going well then bang! - the atmosphere changed. It was nothing I could put me finger on, but I could sense I was being watched. These amateur bastards were trying to set old Rooftop up. So I lie low, do fuck all, then after a couple of weeks the manager calls me in. I get to his office and he's flanked by two auditors. God, I hate them mean mouthed wankers.

The first auditor, he looks like some ex-copper; no recommendation that, if he ain't got the brain to hack it there then he ain't no candidate for Mastermind. The second one is what passes in those circles for a woman. They told me that they had reasonable suspicion to think that a major fraud was taking place and could I help them with their enquiries. I said if it was that serious, they shouldn't be wasting their time chatting to me, they should be out there trying to solve it.

Had to move on after that... another good earner ended. I hated the job anyway, pure abuse; if any idle out of work wanker swore at me he got his case paper

14

filed down the back of a radiator.

It didn't really matter though, cos an old mate of mine from Buckley Hall Detention Centre, a lad called Cooper, got me a job as a barman on the trains. I liked Cooper, he was a car thief and we used to make a butty together. We knew this barber on Moston Lane and he'd give you fifty pence a piece for any music cassette you brought him. Never mind easy listening, this was easy fucking money. We used to walk round the back of Strangeways Prison where all the garment factories are. This was in the days when arseholes used to have little racks of cassettes on their dashboard. I'll tell you, me and Cooper soon put an end to that egalitarian practice. What we'd do is pan the window in with a centre punch, bang all the cassettes in a carrier bag and go see Mr Cut and Blow Dry. Twenty a day was no problem, so we always made our beer money, plus we took the players and anything else we could lay our deviant grubby hands on.

I'd never have met Cooper if it wasn't for Her Majesty's Introduction Service. It's funny that, a lot of the stuff I've been involved in wouldn't have happened if I hadn't been introduced to kindred spirits in HM's different establishments.

Years later when they were rioting on the Strangeways roof, slinging off all the slates and tearing the place to fucking pieces, I went down to watch it from Cheetham Hill Road with Cooper, Robbie and Badger, and I thought to meself, fuck, the first time I met each of these people was in a lock up of some kind.

Anyway, Cooper gets me taken on as a barman on the trains and I'm working with these two Scots lads, both mates of Cooper's dad.

I found the score out the first day; they come up to me sort of intimidating like and the big one says,

-I do the drink - you understand, son?

I didn't but I assured him that I did.

The little one pokes his finger in me chest, stares up me nose, and says,

-And the fucking sandwiches are mine!

I thought I was working with a couple of psychopathical firm's men.

Then I get put on the Edinburgh train with the pair of radgepots and get the gist of their game. It was simple - they sold their own stuff at British Rail prices; they were making a butty in more ways than one. Fair play to them as well - they were offering a wider range, and quality goods.

I've always been a quick learner and willing to do an apprenticeship with the right people, so within days I was part of the team. It didn't last long; we were far too fucking greedy, and one day the Edinburgh train gets met at Manchester Piccadilly by the British Rail police.

I've got to hand it to the Scots lads, they said I was an innocent party but, net result - the sack, and another little earner ended.

If it wasn't a fiddle it was a total fuckabout. I landed a month's work through another mate, a lad called Berty. It was in this sweat shop called the Music Swop in the centre of town. What they did was sell sheet music. They had a shop but the majority of their business was done by mail-order. So that was me main job - upstairs over the shop hunting down Opus this and Opus fucking that all day long. I had to find all the shit on the list, wait for this old twat to do an invoice and then I'd have to parcel them up and post them off. Talk about fucking boring.

The conning bastards had a photocopier, which I knew was against the Copyright Act, but who gives a fuck?

On the Thursday of me final week I was that pissed off that when the old twat gave me the orders to send off, I sent them everywhere I could fucking think of. The Heywood Arms got a load of Mantovani. The Walton

House Men's Hostel got a selection of Beethoven, me Aunty Mary got Woody Guthrie Sings Folk, and I even posted one out to -'Not Known at this Address'.

I got me money on the Friday, told everyone it had been a pleasure working with them. The sad old twat actually bought me a leaving card and put a pound in it. Tuesday comes and I've got Berty banging at me door,

-You're in the shit, he says, they're talking about getting the Police on you. I told them give it a day and I'll see if you'll pay all the post and for anything that's missing. He genuinely looked worried.

-Like fuck, I say; tell them to send the Police. I'll plead guilty, and when the Magistrate asks if there's anything I'd like to say before sentencing, I'll say I did it in protest against the continued contravention of the Copyright Act, and we'll see who's in the shit then.

I heard fuck all after that.

Numerous jobs came and went about this time. I was sort of treading water with no future.

Me main employment was as a shop assistant in dead end jobs. John Collier, the tailor with the window to watch was a fucking scream. It was there that I developed me famous body swerve. What you did was get the customer on the blind side of a rail of suits, make sure it's a cash sale and he's got the exact money. If the suit's £49.99 make it easy on yourself, charge £45 for cash. Leave the customer gazing at himself in the mirror, wander over to the bag dispenser near the till, take a bag, make sure the others are busy. If the big girl on the till is doing her nails as normal you're on the home run. Walk back to your punter, neatly fold his suit, place it in the bag, and wave the cunt off the premises.

-Have a nice day Sir.

Then turn and walk as if to take the money to the till, carefully observing exactly where the manager

Phipps, his assistant Black, and the other two creeping arseholes are. If anybody's watching, take no risks; just ask the big girl to ring a sale - 1% commission instead of 100%. Two choices now - either walk up to Wendy, compliment her on her outfit, chat her up for five minutes; that way, anybody seeing the customer leave will automatically think you're tilling a sale, and as you're staring down her cleavage slide the money into your pocket; or if you're sure all the wankers are too busy to have clocked you, just body swerve the till and head downstairs to either the rest room or the toilet.

The cunt in charge of the place, Phipps - what a bastard! - he ran the place like a fucking slave ship. He was banging Wendy on the till, and if he caught you chatting to her he'd have you outside mopping the step.

Which was totally fucking humiliating. One day I was out there doing that when Big Tony and Sellotape passed - The fucking stick I took....

-Here, says Tony, pointing to his shoes, give these fuckers a shine when you're finished!

One day this old cunt, a regular customer, turns up to have his jacket altered. It was for some fancy fucking club. Phipps is making a fuss of him so I gather he's important. I'm over the other side of the shop, it's dead, fuck all happening, when Phipps shouts,

-Mr Rafferty, will you take this jacket downstairs please and put it with the garments for altering?

We all called each other Mister - supposed to sound professional. I didn't give a fuck. I'd call you God if you left your wallet open near me.

Anyway I'm feeling totally pissed off at the wank wages and the long hours, so I take this cunt's blazer downstairs and decide to rip the piece of shit to pieces. I get a pair of Tailor's scissors and snip off his buttons, then I decide to cashier him from his Regiment, and tear his badge off. After I've had me fun I take the remnants and put them out of the toilet window, out with a load of old shite for the rats to piss on.

A couple of minutes later I'm in the rest room giggling to meself when Wendy comes downstairs.

-Someone's happy, she says.

And walks past me.

Now at this time I'm nineteen and she's about forty. I'm not a bullshitter or much of a womanizer, but the high took over me.

She's walked over to the kettle, and she's washing her cup. She's got on this short skirt and white clingy sort of blouse. Lovely big tits, not a sign of them sagging, and I'm looking at the outline of her bra strap from through the material. Her perfume is nearly knocking me out. I walk up slowly behind her, kiss the back of her neck and slip me hands round over her tits. She gasps but makes no attempt to stop me.

Now there's been very little erotic happened to me in my life, I'm not one of those arseholes who claims to have had three nurses in a train toilet. To me, a woman's clitoris is a bit like Antarctica - I know it's down there somewhere but to be honest I couldn't give a fuck where.

So anyway she turns round; she's a little bit stunned, but she's panting and I'm getting excited cos Phipps is fucking her, and I hate the bastard.

-Come on Wendy, I say, and me hands are all over her tits.

-No, someone might come down, no please, she says. And I'm beginning to think she's asthmatic cos she's panting like fuck.

I've got her blouse undone, me hands are inside her bra and me tongue's trying to count her teeth.

I slowly move her over to the canteen table and push her - she's sat on some fuckers cheese butty. I'm trying to get her legs apart, she's moaning and resisting. My head's buried in the mountain of her tits. Her nipples are rock hard and my cocks even harder, I'll tell you I could've knocked a nail in with it.

-After work, Ronnie, come to me flat; not here, please! she's saying, and she's got a good grip on me arm and I can't prize her knees apart.

-OK, I say - what time?

This reassures her and she loosens the grip on my arms, and I'm between her legs; she's wearing her skirt as a belt now. Her tits are bouncing free and they're bigger and firmer than I thought.

-Six o'clock, she says.

I don't even know where she lives; she hasn't realized it yet, but as the song goes it's now or never.

I'm pulling her knickers down, she's making a futile attempt to stop me but my fingers are up her and she's cross eyed with anticipation.

-What if Phipps comes down? she's saying, but she's adjusting her arse so as to accommodate me as she says it.

-He can bat second, I say and I'm unzipping.

-No Ron, later, please, later, she's murmuring.

But it's too late baby now, and I'm on her giving it to her on the fucking dinner table. There's a cup of mouldy tea bags next to her head. She's squirming and wriggling away and I'm pumping and slavering away. Her big tits are bouncing all over and she's saying,

-Yeah, go on, faster....

Well, I was faster than Damon Hill going for pole position and I come in about a minute and a half.

You should have seen her face - frustrated to fuck. What did she want me to do, light two cigarettes and lie among the tea bags with her?

Anyway, the sad tosser comes back for his jacket the next week. Phipps is everywhere looking for it and the old boy is patient at first. Then he realizes that his precious coat ain't there.

Me an Phipps are downstairs and he's totally lost it.

-Where the fuck did you put it? he's saying.

And I'm making a right pantomime of checking for it. Mr Bossman ain't sussed out that it's gone yet.

He ends up taking a right good arse kicking before giving the old twat another jacket free of charge and making a payment to cover badge and buttons. I'm made up - that'll teach the twat to have me sweeping and mopping like a Mississippi black.

Phipps had it in for me after that. But it didn't really matter, cos I only lasted about another week.

This man and his wife were looking at a suit. Phipps is on his lunch with Wendy, which is sort of ironical, cos I'd been on somebody else's lunch with her a fortnight before. It's a golden opportunity for an earner. So I wander across and say,

-Can I help you Sir?

-How much is this please? he says, taking a suit off the peg.

I look at the label on the back and say,

-It should be forty eight ninety nine but you can have it at sale price, forty pound, Sir.

The plonker hands me the forty pound. I go for a bag, bin the forty, bag his gear and wave him off the premises.

-Thanks for your custom and please call again, Sir.

Mr and Mrs Average fuck off home and I'm thinking it ain't been a bad Picnic at Hanging Rock.

I was wrong - it was about to be a Hanging at Picnic Rock.

They come back a couple of hours later and they're after a refund. Phipps is dealing with them personally. He hates people who renege and return stuff. He takes it very personal. I'm earwigging, hiding behind the ties. Phipps is saying,

-A mark on it Sir? - are you sure it was present when the garment left the shop?

The man's browbeat, but he ain't changing his mind. Phipps says,

-Receipt please? and puts his hand out.

That's when all hell let loose. I can't hear it all cos I've moved right out of the way. But the gist of it is, the man is claiming he paid forty pound cash and didn't get a receipt. Phipps is saying everybody gets a receipt, and no one gets such a generous discount, even during the sale, which incidentally ended five weeks ago. I'm thinking they've both got a point, when the man points over to me and says,

-He served me, ask him.

I start to walk over. There's only one way out of it now and that's to lie like fuck.

-I don't remember him, I say, and for one glorious moment me and Phipps are in harmony - we think we've cornered a Kamikaze shoplifter.

The man's wife is crying.

Then this arsehole called Black walks over, points at me and says,

-I saw you serve him.

And I'm cornered like Brian London against Cassius Clay. The Dirties are called. I could do a runner, but that's as pointless as Manchester City on Derby day. So I'm led away by two uniformed Dirties.

As I'm leaving, Phipps shouts,

-You've brought shame and disgrace to the name of John Collier!

I shout back,

-Don't worry - I'll wear one of your suits in court as an advertisement.

I've never understood cunts like him who think their jobs are important. No twat would even fucking notice if they never turned up again.

Anyway, another earner ended.

Well that gives you a rough idea about me. A character of devious leaning and nefarious intent, as Justice Boyd-Wickens once waxed.

Oh yeah, the nickname Rooftop. I got given that years

before, when I was a teenager. Me and a mate of mine, Dodge Robins, specialised in burgling shops on Rochdale Road. Our Modus Operandi was ripping slates off and going in through the roof. Anyway one day me and Dodge are coming down a fire escape and we land right in front of that rare breed - a member of the Dirty on foot patrol. Well, Dodge who is about six foot two and not much of a runner cuts across Queens Road. Me, who's about five seven and pretty nifty drops the gear I'm carrying and legs it across towards Collyhurst Flats. The Dirty, epitomising the bravery that we all associate with that profession, decides to chase the smaller man, namely me. I get a good head start, lose the arsewipe round a corner, duck into a Maisonette opening and climb down a rubbish chute. I think I'm safe as milk but I'm wrong - I'm about as safe as a drunken knife thrower's sequined assistant.

As he draws level with the opening a cow on the verandah shouts,

-He's gone in the bottom and he hasn't come out the top yet.

I'm cursing the fucking bitch - what business of hers is it? But I'm stuck like a rat in a drainpipe.

Two bits of good advice when dealing with Mr Law Enforcement Officer. One, when you're definitely caught, surrender and two, always tell them exactly what they already know.

So I'm in the Dock ready for sentencing, and the afore mentioned Justice Boyd-Wickens before sentencing me, refers to me as Rooftop Rafferty the Rochdale Road Raffles. A big laugh all round.

Net result - remanded for probation reports and a nickname for life. Though the cunt did give me time six weeks later.

He's dead now, Boyd-Wickens. Which is a pity, cos even though he sent me down he had a sense of humour not often found in them circles.

A couple of years earlier a mate of mine, Jonesy was up before him, and looking like getting serious time. When the Dirty were reading their statements against him they said that when they gained access to Jonesy's flat they found it in darkness and that the only form of light was a series of candles in bottles all around the room. On hearing this Boyd-Wickens stops the case and asks Jonesy,

-Are you a follower of the Prince of Darkness?

Jonesy looks at him puzzled and says,

-I don't understand what you mean.

Boyd-Wickens says in a sombre voice,

-Are you a Satanist?

-Oh no, says Jonesy, I'm a Protestant.

-Glad to hear it, says the Justice, I wouldn't want to be responsible for unearthing a coven in Collyhurst.

And smiles.

Jonesy smiles back and at the end of it comes out with a suspended sentence.

So Wickens wasn't all bad.

MARGERY

At the time of Funny Red Nose day I wasn't married, but I had two and a half kids as Margery was pregnant on our third, little Eammon at the time. We finally called it a draw, kid wise, after the fourth was born, a girl we called Shannon. I married Margery then for two reasons - one I thought it only fair to let her bear my name if she'd gone to the trouble of bearing my babies and two, I found I'd be sixteen quid a month better off with the Tax. So it's Jacksons Row Registry Office and *Heaven Knows I'm Miserable Now* as our song. I started as I meant to go on as well, as soon as I'd finished saying, "I do", I nipped in the Nags Head with two mates for a pint. She only walks in with the four kids and says,

-Come on you, home.

It's a proper show up, so I say,

-Fuck off Margery, I've given you the rest of me life I'm taking the afternoon off.

Anyway, it was a nice touch having the children as Pages and Bridesmaid.

Margery was born in Wythenshawe, a place not renowned for its production of University students, and Margery was no different. She's seven years younger than me and to make matters worse she looks even younger. When she was eight month pregnant with our first, Brendan, I used to take the piss mercilessly. One time we were on a bus going to Blackley and I'm half pissed. She was going on eighteen at the time, but no way would she pass for a day over fourteen. The bus is half full of the usual nosy fucking bastards. What did someone once say? - if you're still getting on a bus at forty you're a failure in life - dead right.

Anyway I start talking loud enough for everyone to hear,

-Just tell me sweetheart, I say.

She looks at me. Doesn't have a clue what's going

on,

-You what? she says.

So I say,

-Me and your mother will stand by you. Who's the father? Is it the black lad off the paper round?

All these arseholes are turning round and tutting. Fuck them, what's their worry? - they're getting free entertainment.

This bit will make you sick, but it was love at first sight. I met her on a blind date. What happened was, I was engaged to this other girl, Dee. Then one day she ups and fucks off with this security guard. It absolutely gutted me; she said she'd had enough of me gambling, drinking and thieving. I said,

-Can't we concentrate on the more positive aspects of my character?

It never even raised a fucking smile.

I'll tell you a rat knows exactly when to leave a sinking ship, it's when it sees a woman packing.

The thing was, it was pride more than anything. When I first met Dee she was a baby-sitter for me mate Dodge. On Friday and Saturday nights me, Dodge and his wife Mary would go out boozing and Dee would mind the kids. I didn't really fancy her, to be honest I didn't really notice her.

Anyway one night we get back and I'm half pissed. Dee goes to bed and Mary starts winding me up about her, saying she fancies me and what have you. So I go upstairs - go into her room. The curtains are open and she's lying on the bed in this big long nightie thing. It looks like Miss Haversham's wedding dress in *Great Expectations*, and speaking of expectations, I had a few meself. I stagger over to her and I startle her. She screams out, thinking I'm gonna rape her. I nearly have a fucking heart attack and I can hear that cow Mary downstairs pissing herself. So I say,

-Sorry Dee - I just wanted a chat.

She sits up and we spend the whole night talking, which ain't hard for me cos I've been on the speed. After that I was fucked; she clung closer than a limpet mine for four long years. Then Mr. Three-Pound-An-Hour came along.

How I got told I was being substituted was a fucking jazzer. She only phones me up and says,

-I've got someone else.

I'm sat in the fucking lobby at me Mam's house. Me head goes and I start to punch in all these little square windows in the front door. It cuts me hand to fuck. I go back to the phone. Me head's been cabbaged.

-It fucking hurts, I say, meaning the pain inside. She only fucking says,

-You shouldn't smash windows then should you?

It was then that I realised that maybe the demise of the relationship wasn't affecting us equally.

Anyway me Dad comes down the stairs sees the broken glass and says,

-What the fuck's going on ?

-I've had some bad news, I say.

-So fucking have I, he says pointing to the windows - the only cunt getting good news round here is the fucking glazier.

What's this all got to do with Margery you're probably wondering? Right - when Dee fucked off and I realised she wasn't coming back I was devastated - I was a laughing stock. We'd been saving for two years for a house and suddenly she's off in a sports car.

I think, right - fuck this, I'm gonna have it out with her. Put her straight and get her back. It wasn't so much that I was missing her, but everybody was taking the piss something chronic. You know the script:

-Why'd she leave you?

-Wanted a bigger prick.

-Yeah well, she won't get a bigger prick than you.

Ha fucking ha!

So this night I go round, I decide to be tough - this is her last chance. When I get there his sports car is only parked outside her bedroom window. She lives in a Tower Block, her old man's the Caretaker and they have a ground floor flat. There's a group of lads coming out of the Apollo pub and I know a couple of them. By now all reason has left me head. All I can think of is her in there with him and I lose it completely. According to the Blackley Gazette I clambered onto the sports car roof. Although a more romantically inclined reporter at the Manchester Evening News described me leaping onto the roof in a dance of destruction. All I'll say is that, if at half past eleven at night after all I'd drank that day, if I was able to leap onto a car roof then some Manchester breweries want suing over the alcohol content of their beer.

Either way, Mr Security Guard comes running out in his bare feet, a state of affairs I was later to be thankful for. I'm still on top of the car like King Kong on top of the Empire State Building, only I'm Fay Wrayless. He draws level with the car and says,

-What's your game?

It took me back a second cos it was such a stupid fucking question. I mean, what the fuck did he think it was? I felt like recommending a course in Mechanics for the thick bastard.

-Nobody fucks my woman, you bastard! I say.

And this brings a roar of approval from the drunks exiting the Apollo. As we stand there I can see all the lights going on in the Tower Block. I suddenly notice how big he is and I'm thinking, why couldn't she fuck off with a midget? But things have gone too far. To be fair he's being pretty reasonable - I've bounced all over his car and insulted his parentage, and all he's done so far is ask a daft question. The stand-off didn't last long - I punched him right in the mouth.

Now there's something I should tell you about me

fighting abilities - a league table would read like this:

RAFFERTY, RONALD

				PUNCHES	
PLAYED	WON	DRAWN	LOST	FOR	AGAINST
320	1	0	319	11	753

As you can see I've only won the one. That was against a kid called Roddy McKelvin, and he later went on to become a Catholic priest so I'm not quite sure if I slapped him around, or he was turning the other fucking cheek.

So to cut a long story short this security guard smacks me silly. Next thing I know is the Dirty turn up and I'm being run in. At first the twat wants me arrested for assault cos I threw the first punch. But the Dirty takes one look at him and one look at me, and decides it's just criminal damage.

Net result - six hundred pounds in fines and compensation.

There the matter would have ended, but them arsewipes at the Evening News decided I could have page seven. I knew it was me without reading a word of the story, and I knew what type of shite it was gonna be just by looking at the headline: FORMER FIANCE'S FLIGHT OF FANCY. When I walked in the Heywood at the night every cunt had a copy. Andy Warhol said fifteen minutes of fame - I got mine all right.

So anyway, back to Margery. Me blind date was the day after the paper came out. We met in a Holt's pub, the Railway. She walked in and I fell in love with her. She was small, with beautiful strawberry blond hair and green eyes. She had a copy of the Manchester Evening News with her so the night's entertainment was guaranteed.

At the end of the night I bought her curry and chips and took her back to Dodges, and as Emily Bronte would say, reader, I married her.

The great thing about Margery is her unquestioning loyalty. She once smashed a glass in me face, but she'd kill anyone else who tried to do it.

When she was seven and a half months pregnant on our second lad Rory, she did a carryout from Laskys using bent ID. She got this fuck off big Sony telly and a video, signs for an extra year's maintenance, and orders a taxi to take her to Withington. She gets half way there and says,

-I've changed me mind, make it Newton Heath.

That morning she went out to collect the Family Allowance and came back with over a grand's worth of stuff. A game girl, but not a natural for going out doing earners because she looked too young; besides, her brain cells are in single figures.

Her and her brother Robbie were from a broken home, and as the old joke goes - they should know, they fucking broke it. As it went, it afforded them a greater amount of freedom than most children get. In short, they were fucking wild.

Margery has this burn on her right hand. When I asked her how it happened she told me to fuck off. Years later I found out from her brother how she got it. Apparently when she was about ten, her Mam was living with this complete psychopath, the sort of sad wanker who gets his kicks from kicking children.

Anyway, this cunt ain't getting his own way over something, so he takes Margery's doll and flings it on the fire. She just walks over to the fire, takes the doll off and puts it out. Burnt her hand but no tears. I'll tell you, with spirit like that you take some keeping down.

The daft thing is that when I heard that story, the thing that amazed me most was not that Margery plunged her hand into a coal fire but that she had a doll in the first place. She's a good mother and great with babies, but no way can I see her having a doll.

So, by going out with Margery I was introduced into a circle of people that included her brother Robbie, her sister 'Sideways', Tommy the Tramp, and a man who uses his personality as a contraceptive - Scots John.

The first time I took Margery anywhere was to see their Robbie in Thorn Cross young offenders centre; he was about eighteen at the time.

I'd done time there meself years before when it was called Appleton Thorn. So right away we forged a common bond. Most of the screws had moved on but the one in the canteen was still there. A mad bastard, but a likeable character called Barrass, he used to line us up and say,

-Come on, I'll fight any fucking one of you.

He must have been in his late fifties at the time.

I had to go into Warrington with him one day. A Scouser called George drove Barrass, me and this total radge pot from Preston called Lyons.

Lyons was doing his full sentence, didn't want any remission. What the fuck he was doing in open nick is beyond me. He used to say,

-When they gave me two years they gave me an oral contract, and I insist that they fulfill it.

The mad cunt was true to his word - he was always losing time.

One of the petty rules was that you weren't allowed to bring your own food out of the dining hall. They'd rather see it thrown to pigs than you eat at your leisure. One day they catch Lyons sneaking two boiled eggs out. Not really sneaking, cos he was fairly indifferent to rules - he just ignored them.

So they put him in front of the Deputy Governor, who says,

-Seven days loss of remission. Anything to say?

Lyons replies,

-Seven days for two eggs? Good job you didn't find the chicken I took out last week.

Anyway this day we're walking through Warrington town centre, going to get the grub. It was a good little number cos it passed a day at the Gulag. That's the worst thing about open nick, the hours. They get you up at the crack of dawn, a quick shower, then it's all in for a mass breakfast. Shitty porridge during the week and a bit of bacon. Cornflakes at weekend. Then it's assemble for your work details. On the camp, or if you're lucky an outside party to Bruge Police Training College and some fit women training to be Dirties. Home for tea and do what you like to up to ten o'clock. Mind you, doing what you like usually means playing fucking snooker unless someone has smuggled something in. So like I say, long hours; before seven in the morning until gone ten. In Strangeways at least you get to sleep it away.

That's why little trips out to Warrington were considered a treat. I even volunteered to take the slops to the pig wagon, which stank of shite. Better than spending one extra minute with some of the cunts I've been banged up with.

So, Barrass has really done the three of us a favour - it's a glorious day - we've got our HMP jumpers tied round the waist and we're in shirt sleeves. Me and George are looking at every bit of skirt under the age of sixty. Lyons is walking behind. I've known him four months and I know he's a Molotov Cocktail waiting for a match. All's well until we cross this bridge over a little river. Barrass turns to tell Lyons to get a move on. As he does so Lyons whips off his boots and throws them in the river. There's stunned silence from the four of us. The barmy ginger headed bastard Lyons just smiles and says,

-Blisters.

-You fucking cunt! yells Barrass, I'll sling you in after them!

But he doesn't, cos he knows it's useless. Barrass has

spent his whole working life in the service and he's seen a thousand Lyons before. They sent him back to Walton after that, he was creating anarchy. People, clocks and regimes can't handle the Lyons of this world; they refuse to be nailed to invisible hands.

Anyway, back to Margery - the first few months were fantastic, non stop screwing. Then suddenly she's pregnant.

I start drinking heavy and gambling what little money we had. It's the usual story, you never win in a Bookies when you need to. When the Gods of Chance see you on the floor bleeding, that's when they start looking for their Doc Martens. I'll tell you, over a short period of months I had every misfortune you could possibly encounter in a fucking bookmakers. Stewards Enquiries, Objections, PhotoFinishes, and during one fucking memorable dog race the hare broke down with mine in front.

Margery's fucking depressed, she's got Post Natal Depression.

So there I am, in debt up to me bloodshot eyes. Behind with me mortgage. On a final warning at work, and I feel like Lemuel Gulliver, a thousand little ropes tying me down. When one night Robbie comes to our house with a cheque book and card. He's gonna sell to a lad called Freddie at four pound a page. I take one look at the signature, decide I can do it, and I'm launched into a Kiting career.

ROBBIE

We got on well together me and Robbie, right from the start. Like I say, me first meeting with him was when he was finishing off eighteen months in Thorn Cross. He'd already done his fair share of time; Approved School, Detention Centre, Borstal and YP - not bad for a teenager! I was thinking of ringing Horace McQuirter and seeing if he qualified for the Guinness Book of Records. When he came out I was living with his sister in a little terrace off Droylsden Road in Newton Heath. Robbie wasn't doing a lot so he used to call down quite a bit.

The first earner we got involved in together was ripping off seaside boarding houses. It was a shit way of earning a crust and the money was wank. What we'd do is fuck off to places like Whitby and Morecambe, dress up smart and sort of casual, and I'd assume the role of Robbie's boss. Then we'd book into a boarding house, carrying two big fuck-off holdalls which would be padded out with wood. I'd tell Robbie to keep shtum, let me do the talking cos every time he opened his mouth he sounded like a Mexican bandit.

I'd walk up to the reception and say,

-Three nights please.

Engage whoever in idle talk. Give them some shit that we were down for whatever, or that we were salesmen. Then I'd sign us in under some name or other. Me main system in choosing bogus names was to rotate the England 1966 World Cup Final team. The thinking behind this was that firstly it was the only football team that me and Robbie both had committed to memory and secondly, if we got a different receptionist from the one who booked us in we wouldn't suddenly go blank and forget our own names. We couldn't use the same name each time cos if the Dirty collar us we've done the hard work for them. Plus there was always the chance of one of the boarding houses phoning ahead to another, warning of a Mr Charlton working the area. So a change of name each time seemed like a good idea. It worked great until the fourth one we did in Yarmouth one Bank Holiday.

Anyway, we'd be at the desk booking in,

-Two rooms please, single, I'd say.

-Names please?

-Oh just put them under my name, Mr R.Wilson, please.

Then the sting ...lift up the holdall and say,

-Is there a launderette near for these things?

The bag's padded so it looks like it's got twenty pound worth of weight in it instead of two sticks.

They'd give you directions or tell you to ask in the High Street. Grab a leaflet of the local attractions; as you're going, say,

-Is there a shower on our floor?

That keeps them from being nosy, cos they think your first intention is to shower.

Then go up to your rooms, take the wood out of the holdalls, bang a television in each. Grab anything else worth a few fucking bob. Any luck and there will be a drinks cabinet. If not, you might cop for a pay telephone in the hall. Then walk back downstairs, making the weight of the bags look similar to the weight you brought in.

If you're clocked going out just wave and say,

-Launderette in Capstan Street you say? - see you later.

Out the door, round the corner, in the car, and it's Hi Ho Silver and away, don't wait for no thanks.

Like I say, Yarmouth was a complete balls up. We'd already done three, so I'm at the reception booking in at our fourth. It's late and the place is hammered - they've only got one room left and it will be ready in half an hour. I sign in, say I'll keep the bags with us cos we need things out of them.

We go away, have a quick pint, come back forty minutes later. Robbie goes to the counter, comes back and he says,

-We're not booked in.

I look at him and say,

-Course we fucking are, you saw me do it.

The people at the reception desk, two middle aged fuckers are staring at us and muttering.

-No fucking Moore on their lists, he says.

-Moore? I say, I booked in under Stiles. This is our fourth - Stiles wore number four. Bobby Moore was six.

-Like fuck! says Robbie.

We're attracting suspect stares so we abort the mission and fuck off, arguing.

I fucking hated it though, there was never any real money in it. If you motored far you had to do six or eight in a weekend to make it pay.

We got twenty five to thirty for the tellies depending on age, sometimes less, from Smart Bargains in Clayton. The pay phones we broke the locks off and emptied. Scots John gave us a fiver each for the bust phones. We thought he was fucking up cos the locks were shagged and we didn't have any keys.

We found out later that the tricky cunt knew a locksmith, got new locks and keys done at three pound a piece and then sold them off through the Loot at forty odd a time. I hate that twat, but you've got to admire his front.

The thing that got me the most about it all was that I actually liked most of the landladies. They were supplying a good cheap service, scratching along out of season earning a shit living. Then me and the Ringo Kid hit town and a week's profits gone. We must have made some very nice people cynical and bitter. I jacked it in after a couple of weeks - left Robbie and Scots John to it. I signed off the sick and went back to the

Council, wiping mechanic's arses.

I started watching a few City matches with him after that. I'm a Bolton fan so shit football's never bothered me. I only went to the away games to get a pint out of town and maybe a bit of a nobble.

I remember one game, Ipswich away it was, just after the high winds and what have you had ripped fuck out of the East Coast. The place was fucking devastated, trees uprooted, the monty. Seven of us piled into a shagged- out old estate car. It became a weekend of non-stop shoplifting. The main men being me, Robbie and a lad called Tommy the Tramp. I was out of me league.

The thing was you just couldn't beat Tommy - cos he just couldn't give a fuck, and took for taking's sake. We pulled into a little Suffolk village, fuck all there, just a few shops. The biggest crime they'd ever seen was the theft of garden gnomes. Me and Tommy decide we want a scran. The trouble with football weekends, you didn't know when you were gonna eat next so you grabbed what you could when you could. Anyway, we go into this country pie shop, a friendly little place. There's an old girl serving and she's chatting to two middle aged women. Tommy walks straight between the women, gives everyone his big Jack Nicholson smile, stares at the pies and says,

-I'll tell you what Mother, those pasties look lovely - give us two hot ones for out.

The woman delicately puts them in a bag using tongs, passes Tommy the bag, smiles and says,

-Two twenty please.

Tommy just turns and walks out. The poor girl doesn't have a clue what the twat's doing.

As he gets to the door she shouts after him,

-Excuse me, you haven't paid!

The three women in the shop are silent - they're in a state of total shock.

The old girl turns to her friends and says,

-What can I do? - my till will be down.

I feel sorry for her; she's had her day ruined.

The two girls in front of me move aside, they're in no hurry, their fucking afternoon gossip's just been sorted.

-Two of them pasties please, I say.

A look of absolute fear comes across her face. She thinks she's about to get turned over twice in a minute.

She bags the pasties for me but keeps hold of them while she's asking for the money. It's a sort of Mexican stand-off as we do the exchange.

It's sad - her whole fucking faith in humanity has been destroyed for less than three pound. For that trivial amount, she's moving onto Paranoia Street with the rest of us.

I've got a few bob on me and I'm getting fucking soft, so I say,

-Take for four please. He's been very ill since his mother died. He doesn't know what he's doing.

The atmosphere immediately leaves the shop. The two ladies smile and the old girl behind the counter says,

-Oh poor thing - I'm sorry, I didn't realise.

I smile and leave. It's fucking nice to be nice.

I stroll back to the car and I'm thinking -did you clock that one God? Dust the book down and get that one down in the credits.

When I get back to the car it looks like it's been packed by the Nawab of Bengal as a dress rehearsal for the Black Hole job he did in Calcutta.

Tommy sees me pasties and he's full of admiration.

-Fuck me, he says, silly old cow fell for it twice.

-Yeah, I say - silly old cow.

He was a character, Tommy was; he stopped shaving when his mother died. He cultivated this wild beard and even wilder sense of humour. His speciality was

Aggressive Begging. He'd walk up to people and speak right into their faces,

-Only you got to eat today? Don't I fucking count?

It was incredibly successful. One day we're waiting in Piccadilly for Robbie; we're next to the phone boxes, then out of the blue he starts begging. I fucked off away from him. There's this well dressed man going into one of the boxes. Tommy stands in his way and says,

-Make it a short call Uncle, give me what you've got left.

Another young lad he buttonholes with,

-No Big Issues left, Nephew, but I've still got to eat.

He had this menacing stare and threatening way of coming at people. If they tried to divert round him he'd yell,

-Oh, taking the outside lane are you? That's it, don't meet me eyes! Don't think about me kids!

He stops this young girl about nineteen, and she's frightened stiff of him. He's breathing in her face and she's embarrassed and scared.

-Give us the price of a Holland's meat pie, he says, taking off a cheap market watch, -you can have me ticker but give me some fucking money.

Poor cow is wetting herself with fear - she delves in her bag and gives him two quid in change.

I got into a good little earner with Robbie and Tommy the Tramp. I'd been on the sick for a couple of months with me back but I was pissed off with it, so I signed off and went back to work.

When I got back they put me on this new initiative, called the Alcohol Policy.

Let me tell you about the City Council - it's ran by the biggest load of arseholes this side of Liverpool. New fucking policies every fortnight - Dress Code Policy, Equal Opportunities Policy, Drink Policy, No Smoking Policy - you name it, they had it!

The Equal Opportunities one really pissed me off. I

didn't need no pamphlet written by no Town Hall arse bandit to teach me what me Dad taught me at the age of ten.

He'd heard me call this black kid a nigger. He slapped me head right off me shoulders and took me in the house. Then he explained to me about when he came to England in the nineteen thirties from Dublin. He went looking for work and he sees signs on factories that say,

-No Irish employed here.

He said that someone had written underneath one of them,

-The same is written on the gates of Hell.

So me Dad told me that he'd been the Englishman's nigger, and that it wasn't very pleasant to hear forty years of jokes about his stupidity by men who'd never read a single book. Told me that he'd worked with men for over a decade who still called him Paddy cos they were too stupid or ignorant to learn the name Eugene. After that I stopped being English, and I've never insulted a man for his colour since.

One of the most sorted men I ever worked with was this Indian lad (the sort that John Wayne didn't kill), Avinash. We worked together in a bar off St Anne's Square and the earner that we had going each week was a dozen bottles of Double Diamond apiece. He didn't drink so he gave his share to me, and he never accepted any money in return. So he was risking his job just the same as me for fuck all. Like I say, a sorted lad. He left his coat out the back one day and his wallet was in it, so I dipped him for forty quid. It was nothing personal; I'd have done it if he was white.

Anyway the Alcohol Policy comes out, and I read the document. There's no proper guidelines for management to keep a check on you. So I immediately sign on and it's happy motoring for a good piss take.

Every Friday afternoon I go to see this fucking

40

bleeding-heart on Oldham Street. I spend an hour, one till two, with her filling out me drinks diary and me telling her any shit that comes into me head. Ten past two I'm in the Smithfield Vaults having a pint and a game of pool. I'll tell you, they gave me every Friday afternoon off with full pay for eighteen months. They paid me to get pissed in an attempt to stop me getting pissed.

The best part of it though was these two geriatrics they sent down from the Union Central Office. Real nice old farts, Harry and Bert they were called, the same names as Captain Pugwash's henchmen in the cartoon. Harry showed a real interest in me financial problems while Bert was more interested in whether I beat the wife and forced her to have sex. I cheered the old fucker up. I told him I stripped her naked and had sex with her in front of the kids. A load of bollocks - as if I'd dare raise a hand to her - she'd knife me if I tried! But it all made good theatre for Bert.

Harry was me man though. What I did was accumulate some bills showing that I was in debt up to the eyeballs and get the old cunt to agree a five hundred pound interest free union loan. I was supposed to pay the loan back at twenty five a month. As if. I paid the first instalment back, that way they can't do you for fraud cos I can prove an original intent to pay, then I cancel the Direct Debit. Fuck the Tolpuddle Martyrs.

Harry lost interest in me after that. Bert stopped visiting when I told him that Margery had left to form a lesbian relationship with a Sri Lankan.

Anyway, me good little earner with Robbie and Tommy - it all began as a drunken piss about. We'd been to watch City lose at home to Palace, three one. City had been winning but their keeper threw a wobbler and got himself sent off for punching a Palace player. He should have done it in the tunnel not on the pitch. After the game the aggravation, as the football press usually says, boiled over on to the terraces and we have a bit of a mini riot. The usual; lob a few bricks through a few coach windows, chant for Swales to get sacked, get chased by the Dirty and end up in the City Social Club. We grab a couple of pints and we listen to Bob Reilly, a Miles Platting Blue (not many of them about), tell us about his latest conquest. He's a great story teller Bob, he could make the weather forecast sound funny. He's not missed a City game in years.

I once bumped into him in a pub in Bolton, the day of the Nat Lofthouse Testimonial. We're both there to support different teams as the Wanderers are me first love, but we team up for a drink. We have a good session and come out of the King William about fifteen minutes before kick off. As we get out there's about thirty Bolton lads kicking shit out of five or six City boys. All we have to do is cross the Manchester Road and we're in the Old Railway Embankment, the one they turned into a supermarket.

But no, Bob can't leave his compatriots and shouts,

-Come on you Blues! and wades in.

Me, I get a lump of wood over me head from a fellow Bolton fan and wake up in hospital.

I get back to Manchester the next day and Bob's translated my part in it into Audie Murphy in *The Red Badge of Courage*.

Anyway we finish our beer with Bob, and me, Robbie and Tommy taxi it to town. It's late Christmas shopping and I've promised to get me oldest, Brendan, a Lego Police Station. Don't know why he wants one of them, he'll see enough of the real ones when he's older. So we are outside Toys-R-Us behaving like Dickheads-R-Us. The set's in the window for thirty three pound. Tommy says,

-Fuck me Rooftop, you ain't paying that! Give us a tenner and I'll go in and get it.

-The job's yours, I say.

And he walks in, walks to the shelf behind the window and he starts miming -Flora - like on the advert, and I think he's just fucking about. Then he picks up the box, makes sure there's no little metal alarm on it. If there is all you do is put silver paper over it anyway. Looks at us and walks straight out.

Robbie walks in as he's walking out and gets one as well.

That was the start of it. I get to work on Monday and I tell everyone that me niece has just started at a toy store and she can get any toy on the Market for roughly two thirds of the shop price.

Now remember I'm talking mechanics here - fucking extras from the Living Dead in the Manchester Morgue. The orders roll in. Robbie and Tommy are shoplifting to order. I pay them dead on a third of what's on the box, so I'm making as much as them without getting me hands dirty.

I used to have a toy store catalogue in me desk; I'll tell you what, me and the mechanics consulted it more times than the car manuals. If I didn't like the punter, and I didn't like most of them, I'd say,

-I can get that but I can't really get one third off. What if I got say six quid off? Silly fuckers always said yes.

Something I've always found in life is that all men are thieves but they come in two categories. Thieves with bottle and thieves without bottle. The ones with bottle go out there and steal it, and the ones without buy it off the ones with.

You watch the greedy fuckers in the pub on a Saturday dinner if someone brings a box of bent watches in. They're on him like a bunch of fucking Jackals. Yet if the same poor sod gets caught and sent down, they'll be sat in the same pub come Saturday dinner saying,

-Deserved it, the thieving bastard.

Then they'll look at their watches and see if they've time for another pint.

The toy thing went on for six months then the inevitable happened. Tommy got caught with a sixty pound doll in Kendals. All the arsehole I was getting it for was concerned about was, it fucked up his daughter's birthday cos he'd promised it her and he didn't have the sixty to buy it. I said,

-No problem - third floor Debenhams, near the lifts, go and steal one!

Robbie quit the hop-slifting after that as well, not enough in it for him.

So, as they say, another nice little earner ended.

It might sound like a piss take but Robbie was a good hearted kid. Try telling that to some of the cunts he'd robbed, but it's basically true. The poor cunt never really got taught much else. No tosser was putting his name down for Eton at birth, though it's safe to assume that fate was on the phone to Hindley Borstal. In the game of life every net and line call had gone against him.

I remember one story that sums the mad fucker up. He only turns up at me house one day with a fucking bird table. I mean, a fucking bird table! I lived in a two up two down.

It looks the part - a fuck off big wooden thing, oak or something, with a house on top and a Robin carved on it.

-What the fuck you doing with that? I say.

He smiles and says all proud,

-It's for you, Rooftop.

And stands back admiring the thing.

-Like fuck it is, I say - What the fuck am I supposed to do with it?

-I don't want nothing for it, he says all fucking hurt, -you can put it in your backyard.

-What? I say, and have me windows covered in pigeon

shit? You can shift the shite now.

-Fuck, Rooftop, he says, I've just had to get in a garden in Woodhouses for this. Dog nearly had me and I've done me bollocks in carrying the fucker.

-Do I look like the fucking Birdman of Beswick? I say, - Who'd play me in the film ? Bert cunting Lancaster? Shift the fucker.

-Right, he says and I know I've made him feel a cunt.

I shut the door, go inside, and he fucks off.

-Who was it? says Margery.

-Just some cunt selling bird tables on the drip, I say.

-Oh, she says, did you order one?

And I make a mental note to ring up the *Lancet* to see if there's any doctor doing a thesis on congenital idiocy who'd be interested in the spare bedroom for a month.

Next morning I get up to go for me *Sporting Life* and I see the Bird Table about four houses down. Two neighbours are debating it.

As I pass, one says to the other,

-I don't know - I went to bed last night, nothing there, woke up this morning to this.

The other neighbour is stood there shaking his head in wonder.

-Aliens, I suggest and walk on by.

And Newton Heath had a mystery to rival corn circles.

HEARTBREAK HOTEL

It's funny really, but the most depressed I've ever been was probably the time I had the most fun. When Dee fucked off with the Security Guard, me head was gone for a couple of month before I got meself together and went trampolining on the bonnet of his car. All I did was walk about in a daze or write to her begging her to come back. I phoned her constantly but she wouldn't come to the phone.

Then me mate Dodge's wife Mary left him. She'd gone on holiday to Spain, met some smooth talking London wanker and decided that the other man's grass is greener. When she came back she packed her bags and said goodbye to the Circus.

So with me and Dodge being in the same boat I moved in with him as a lodger. He lived in a terrace in Harpurhey; an Irish lad, Willie Hooley, christened the place Heartbreak Hotel. It became a Mecca for larger than life characters. Anyone wanting to fuck off from their wife for a couple of days sabbatical just turned up there. Big Tony moved in for a couple of nights, and stayed the duration. Irish Joe lived round the corner but was never away and Norfolk Danny, on the run from the Dirty, had a couple of month there before fucking off back down South.

I was loaded cos I'd been saving for a house for two fucking years. So I had fuck all better to do than booze all me savings. I started hammering the sick at work and hung round the house in a depressed state most of the day.

We never watched telly in Heartbreak, just the odd video. All we seemed to do was batter down the drink and play darts. Darts decided everything. Who went to the chippy, who went to the off-license, who put the bets on. Big Tony was barred from going for the videos. I loved gangster films, the older the better; Dodge loved all this Schwarzenegger shit and Irish Joe loved anything with music in it.

Despite our preferences Tony always came back with titles like *Trucking Girls of Bangkok* or *Nympho Schoolies Get Naughty (Starring Seymour Kuntz and Tracey Swallows)*. He claimed the Paki in the shop said it had a good story to it. Nice man that guy, he called himself Jim; I suppose he got more customers and less vandalism by Anglicising it; always let us have tick if we couldn't pay. There always seemed to be more staff than punters. I suppose we were his best customers. We bumped him for forty quid the day Dodge moved out of Heartbreak Hotel. Shame really, cos he was all right. Dodge was like me, on a permanent downer, him more so cos he missed his kids. I swore at first that I was through with women, but Dodge right from the start was having a different one every night.

One day Dodge comes into the living room. Me and Tony are throwing darts. Irish Joe is doing the *Daily Mirror* crossword. Dodge storms in, turns the video off and says,

-Right you bunch of twats, which dirty cunt has been wiping his arse on the toilet wall?

There's immediate uproar.

Irish Joe is first in to defend his honour. He only lives around the corner and he claims if he needs a shit he just nips home. Which, he says, can be a tricky operation because he has a very bad case of the piles. No visual evidence was called for to substantiate his claim.

Me and Dodge go back to before we were even teenagers, in the days when we hid in the Pack Horse false chimney and came out after closing and robbed the place. So me word is immediately accepted.

All eyes turn to Big Tony.

-It ain't fucking me, he says.

There's dead silence, you could have heard a

cockroach fart. Then he adds,

-I always take a newspaper in with me. If there ain't no fucking paper I use that.

He points to Dodge in self defence and says.

-What about you? I ain't seen you take no newspaper in.

Dodge says,

-I don't fucking need to, I always use the green sponge.

Tony looks at him gob smacked, and says,

-You dirty bastard - I've been wiping me face with that for three fucking months.

We all fall about laughing.

Net result - I stop wiping me arse on the wall, and I certainly gave the green sponge a wide berth afterwards.

Another time, Norfolk Danny brings back this pissed up teenager and talks her into playing strip darts. She can hardly hit the board she's that pissed, and Danny is second only to Dodge. All the game she's laughing and drinking extra strong cider. Me, Irish Joe, Tony and Dodge are cheering them on. In no time she's down to her knickers. She's got little tennis ball tits, no bounce, just a ripple when she throws a dart. Danny ain't giving her a chance, he's got his hand down her knickers every time she tries to sling an arrow. She's giggling and loving it and it's even money a gang bang.

Norfolk Danny needs double eight and she's birthdayed. Then it happens. She starts crying, tells us she's fifteen and has run away from home. I'll tell you, by the time she'd finished her story me, Big Tony, Dodge and Irish Joe were in the Kestrel having a pint. We didn't fancy the beasts wing at Strangeways. People pissing in your food and kicking shit out of you. I never did find out if Norfolk Danny knobbed her.

I seen the same girl about two years later in Yates's on Cross Street. I was sat in there with Robbie and his brother-in-law, Freddie. She came in with a group of girls. She was still the same, had to be the loudest of the bunch. But credit where credit's due, she'd blossomed into a fair looking girl and her tits were now more like rugby balls than tennis balls. After about half an hour I'm at the bar and she comes up. So I let on to her and she blanks me. I go back to our table and tell the lads where I know her from. We have a laugh about it and I can see her sort of staring over - maybe she remembers, and maybe she don't. As Freddie's going to the toilet he passes her and says,

-Do you still play darts?

You should've seen the look on her face. Her eyes begged him not to say anything in front of her friends. Fair play to Freddie, he didn't.

The German was a classic. Dodge picked her up one night in the Heywood when he was with Badger. She was one of the most screwed up fuckers I ever come across. She had three small children yet she used to stay out days on end and leave the kids being minded by thirteen and fourteen year olds. When she got her family allowance on a Monday, she used to take men out and didn't come home till it was spent.

I remember one fucking time she calls round to Heartbreak; picks up me, Norfolk Danny and Dodge. We don't want to play out but she says the Milky Bars are on her so we're persuaded. Anyway we have a blitz on her Monday money. Do the pubs along Oldham Road - Copenhagen, Dead House, Boilermakers, Swan, White Hart and finish up in the Spanking Rodger (known locally as the Wanking Lodger). All the way she's funding the outing and it's jukebox, top shelf and "have one yourself".

Then we decide to go back to her place with a carry out. Dodge and Danny get her under the bridge on Collyhurst street and they get her tits out of her blouse. She's just stood there giggling. The traffic's whistling by like it's Le Mans and she's wiggling her assets at them.

-Not bad for a woman touching forty are they? she's shouting, and I've got to agree.

Anyway we walk back to her house, it's about midnight and we've been out since early morning. She's ain't even bothered to put her tits back in her blouse. She puts the key in the door, opens it and says,

-One at a time.

I'm not sure if she's talking about entering her or the house. It's in total darkness. She clicks on the light. Fuck all happens.

-Kiddies, she shouts, tits swinging everywhere, it's Mammy.

A kid of about ten comes out of the darkness. It's her eldest son Travis.

-Mam, he says, there's no electric, it went at dinner time.

And it's one of them times when you're glad to fuck you're not stood in front of a mirror, cos could you fuck meet your eyes. Her house was like Crewe Railway Station.

One day I'm sat in her living room with half a dozen Newcastle Browns. Dodge was upstairs screwing her. You could hear them on the job. She had a fucking lisp and she's saying,

-Go on you clunt, that's it, yeth, I wuv you!

God, it was fucking embarrassing; she must have gone to the Elmer Fudd School of Speech.

All of a sudden the door bangs and in walks her ex-husband. He's a big mean fucker and he's drunk, and for some absurd reason he still loves her. He takes one look at me and he says,

-Oh, they're fucking queuing now are they?

I assume this to be rhetorical, so I say fuck all. The only way out is past him. But there ain't no way I'm getting up in case he misinterprets any sudden movement as a willingness to fight on my part.

The noise from upstairs seems to be getting louder. He's listening to that but he's looking at me. The German is growing excited,

-Yeth, she's saying, yeth go on!

He picks up a picture of his children, smashes it on the edge of a cabinet and slings it at me feet. If that's a gauntlet he can fucking shove it. He starts clenching and unclenching his fists. I prefer the latter part, and I'm praying he learnt the art of pugilism at the same school of boxing as Roddy McKelvin.

Then he says,

-Have you read Plato's Dialogues?

I felt like saying no, I don't read other peoples mail; but I settled for saying just,

-No.

Tears are in his eyes as he says,

-I fucking have. You know what Plato said a man losing his sexual urge was like?

This is getting well out of fucking hand, I'm thinking. I wish that twat would hurry up and finish on the job, then he can come downstairs and take his own hammering, instead of letting me cop for it.

-No, I say.

-Like dismounting a wild horse -

He pauses then he adds,

-Have you ever mounted that wild horse upstairs?

He's rocking back and forth about three feet from me and the tears are flowing.

-Me? I squeal, then the way out of it hits me, and it ain't past him. I raise me voice in indignation and say,

-Listen, I'm not used to discussing my sexuality with strangers, but if you must know I'm gay and I'm in a long term loving relationship at the moment, so in answer to your question, no.

He's knocked out of his stride. We stare at each other in silence. I feel sorry for him. He feels like I felt when

I found out Mr Security Guard was having rumpy pumpy with me fiancee. The poor bastard's being publicly crucified.

The silence is broken by the sounds of lovers in love,
-Suck it German, suck it!

The German makes some weird noises, I'm not sure if she's slurping or lisping.

I look at him, he's calming down. I say,
-Have a Newcastle Brown, tell me about this Plato fella.

Home Brew days became legendary. But a little bit wild - after the first one, the house next door went up for sale.

What we did was me, Dodge, Tony and Irish Joe all bought two forty pint home brew kits and put them on at the same time. Then I got this typist at work, Sylvia, to type me up an invitation—

MESSRS ROBINS, RAFFERTY, HOOLEY AND NICHOLLS REQUEST YOUR PRESENCE AT A BEER TASTING FEST. TO TAKE PLACE AT HEARTBREAK HOTEL AT 10.00AM ON —/—/—. FEATURING A CELEBRATION OF 60'S MUSIC AND BEST, LAW AND CHARLTON VIDEOS

I photocopied it thirty times and entrance was by invitation only. They were out-of-it parties - what we'd do is buy a couple of bottles of spirits, some cider, throw in a bit of fruit and make a punch. The secret ingredients were supplied by a Collyhurst pill head called Johnny Wright. I ain't got a clue what he put in it, but after about three you spoke like Wurzel fucking Gummidge. The parties seemed to go on forever, and usually finished with a twenty a side game of football in the street.

There were these Geordie twins that we met in Blackpool, they used to come down for the parties. Jill and Jan they were called. Identical. I couldn't tell who I was fucking. Dodge reckoned it was easy - Jill gave a gobble, Jan didn't. One time I walked into the bedroom and one of them is bouncing up and down on Tony who's got a can of extra strong cider in his hand, and the other is sat naked doing a crossword, waiting for her turn. It was just like she was in a doctor's surgery. When I walk in she looks up and says,

-What's another word for powerful man?

Anyway, it must have been round about the third Home Brew day. By now things had got right out of hand. We couldn't get any daylight in the upstairs windows for all the For Sale signs going up opposite.

The neighbours got up a petition and all the local shops with the exception of Jim the Pakistani had started to refuse to serve us.

Anyway, this day the party was well out of control. There was a gang of gatecrashers from Monsall in the kitchen, supping all the beer. The cunts hadn't even brought any of their own. They were handy lads and well pissed, and even though we had them out numbered about four to one you could still cut the atmosphere with a Stanley knife.

After a few drinks the tension dies down a bit, and the conversation comes round to football, which together with fucking is common ground. Then it goes off - there's a load of screaming coming from the bathroom. Dodge, Tony and me dash through. When we get there, this Monsall arsehole with FUCK YOUS tattooed on his knuckles has got Jill or Jan, impossible to say which as he wasn't getting a gobble, bent over the toilet bowl. He's attempting to give it her from behind. She's struggling and screaming her head off. Her knickers and skirt are ripped and her head's smacking against the radiator.

It now becomes a matter of honour.

Dodge pulls the Monsall wanker off and says,

53

-Who invited you?

A fairly stupid question, I'm thinking.

-I'm a friend of one of the gatecrashers, the Monsall would-be rapist says, and butts Dodge.

Dodge grabs him and they roll into the kitchen locked in an embrace.

It goes off royal. I pull Jill or Jan back into the toilet and lock the door. The fight's in full swing outside.

Age old rivalries between Miles Platting, Collyhurst and Monsall are being played out with the house as a battlefield. Like I say, I'm a Cheetham boy so I feel honour bound not to interfere with something that ain't none of me business.

It all had to end, and it did. Mary's holiday romance ended and she returned home with the kids. Dodge hummed and harred but he had them back. Which meant that me and the rest had to find alternative accommodation. So I fucked off home to me Mams. Dodge settled back down and he was never his old self afterwards.

Then one night not many months later, Margery told me she was pregnant and that fucked me good style, and I suppose you could say I was never me old self again afterwards either.

Funny to fuck how Margery found out she was in possession of me heir apparent. Johnny Wright told her one night as we sat in the Chieftan stand at Belle Vue Dogs. It was while we were waiting for the result of the fourth race. It had gone to a photo and I'd had twenty on the Two at Threes. Sounds like a fucking Marx Brothers routine that. Still whatever, I'm sweating on the twat to pull me out of the shit.

Then Johnny drags Margery to one side and starts telling her she's expecting. Now let me tell you something about Johnny - he wasn't no Doctor or nothing (though he'd handed out more tablets than most) - how he'd found out was at the time he was knobbing Margery's sister, the Obnoxious Sideways (like that cunt Bede was Venerable and that wanker Ethelred was Unready, that bitch Sideways was Obnoxious) and she'd told him.

Again, like I said about Johnny, Sideways wasn't no fucking doctor either, though she'd changed a shitty nappy or two in her time and claimed to be a nurse. Mind you, at the time Gary Birtles was claiming to be a fucking football player so that didn't mean shit to me. Now you're probably wondering how the fuck did a nappy nurse know about the wonderful gift of motherhood, that the inventor of snot (right in there day six or something, God thinks to himself "OK I've done light, earth, man and what have you - what about a little bit of snot to keep the cunt going?") had bestowed upon her loving baby sister. Simple- Alice, Margery's mother had opened her daughter's hospital letter and told every cunt in Collyhurst the good news. It about sums up Margery's tattered home life - she learns fourth hand at a fifth rate dog track of the most significant event in her life. Sometimes life can be a right fucking bastard.

Anyway, Margery comes back from talking to Johnny. I'm staring at the board wondering which dog's got the fucker. Dodge is certain.

-Yours held on, Rooftop, it's got it by a Scouser's intellect.

When Margery tugs at me jumper like a little kid trying to get her Mother's attention.

-Ronnie, I've got something to tell you, she says.

-Fuck off will you? I say, can't it fucking wait?

She looks at me like she's about to cry, so I say sort of all soft.

-Come here, give us a cuddle, what is it baby?

God, I didn't realise how close to the fucking mark I was.

She starts to tell me,

-Ronnie, it's like.........well..........Johnny says I'm pregnant.

This knocks me fucking backwards, I mean for fuck's sake - "Johnny says"-we went to the same school together and that cunt was worse at biology than I fucking was. How the fuck's he know? Read the fucking tea leaves? Got a message through from his Indian spirit guide, Billy Two-Giros ?

I'm mulling over all this shit when the the bing-bong says,

-Result of photo-finish....first trap two !

Margery's staring at me face to see how I take the news of impending Fatherhood.

-HAHA YES !!! I shout.

And the daft thing is that I meant it on both fucking counts. I wanted the dog to win, and I was chuffed to fuck about having a sprog on the way.

Firing fucking blanks? I'm a loaded and primed fucking cannon.

Cigars and cheap brandy all round.

CLARISSA

Anyway, back to the story. Robbie's girlfriend is Clarissa. She's a belting girl, pure Miles Platting. She's tall and slim, and she took to Kiting like a Scouser takes to rifling purses.

Like the time we were Kiting in Wigan. The team was me to do the male cheques, Clarissa to do the female and Robbie as Driver and Bagman. Before we kick off on the business in hand we go to this town centre pub. I order a pint of bitter each for me and Robbie and a Coke for Clarissa. I take the top off me pint. Me nerves are shattered, I was sick on the way, violently down the side of the Escort. I told them it was a hangover, but if I'm honest it's the fear of Kiting that does it. It's a twat of an earner and to be truthful I know it ain't me fucking game. But I'm such a greedy little cunt that I can't resist the money. I've got a book and a card for a T. Hopkins - it's a real shitter of a signature to get right. I've had the book over the weekend and I've practised the signature a couple of thousand times. I'm starting to think the cunt is left handed, the way he does his K's. I try it again a couple of times more on a beer mat but it don't look right. I tear the fucking mat up. It might sound paranoid, but I don't want to see the bastard again as Exhibit A in The Crown versus Rafferty.

Clarissa says,

-Don't worry Rooftop, it's sorted.

Robbie leans over takes a long look and laughs,

-Like fuck! - he'll be in Risley for tea.

That's all I fucking need, as if I ain't fucking well screwed up enough as it is.

Clarissa's got a book as well and the idea is that we rotate. I do a cheque, come back, Clarissa does a cheque, comes back. Robbie takes the produce to the car. It's supposed to be a real Blitzing operation.

We'd tossed a coin beforehand for who went first. It

came up tails and I'm going first. Her book's in the name of Singh, which ain't so bad for a woman because plenty of white women marry Pakistanis or Indians.

That bastard Scots John sold me a book and a card when I was pissed once. When I woke up the next morning and looked at it, the name was only Mr fucking Patel. I mean, what fucking chance did I have of Kiting that?

Anyway, we'd borrowed Norfolk Danny's van so the transport is sorted. Our aim is to do about five shops apiece, the same five where possible, and on the way home do as many swopsies as we can.

Robbie is the Bagman, all he needs to do is walk in another branch of the same store that we Kited in the morning and say,

-The wife bought this in your Wigan store, got it home and it didn't fit.

Then its ding ding - forty odd pound return.

Anything we like we keep. I liked to get Margery or the kids something while I'm out. That way I'm flavour of the month when I return home.

I kick off in British Home Stores. It's empty. As I'm walking through I'm weighing up the staff. There's two. The first's an old girl who looks as if she flew with Bomber Harris. She's smartly dressed in a bluish uniform and looks a firm's person. No fucking chance I'm going to her.

So I wander through the Sports Jackets. I'm the only fucking customer, which is shite, cos the busier they are the less time they can afford to spend checking the signature.

At the other end of the counter is the second assistant, a young girl, whose left tit has a little sticker saying 'Janine'. I've worked in enough shops to know when an assistant hates her job and let me tell you, just by looking I could tell that Janine fucking hated hers, and she hated Bomber Harris's mother too.

So I'm thinking you'll do for me, as soon as Mrs Slocombe's busy. To kill time I pick up two pairs of trousers, twenty four ninety nine each, as near to the fifty pound card limit as possible. I walk across to the cubicle to try them on. It's amazing, but even when you're doing the swopsie you still always pick clothes that are your own size. I suppose it's conditioning, and I'm in the cubicle thinking about the people clock.

Me brother Eammon told me about it. He said that all human beings worked to an imaginary clock. They had to be at certain places at certain times. It's like at work - tea break, ten till ten past ten in the morning. Dinner, twelve till one. Tea break in the afternoon, three till ten past three. It's all about conditioning.

When he first told me about it I thought he was up it. But the next day at seven sixteen I'm waiting outside the Robin Hood for me lift to work and a British Telecom van drives past and I thought, only five minutes now and me lift will be here. Then it fucking hit me. Murray would pull up at seven twenty one. In the five minutes in between, the fat lady would finish walking her dog in Brookdale Park, pass by and ignore me. The paper girl with the runny nose would put the *Sun* through the door opposite and if it was a Friday, only a Friday, the beautiful Chinese girl with the long legs would smile at me and say,

-Morning, and make me throat run dry.

Eammon was right, the bastards had me chained to the invisible hands of a giant clock. The whole of humanity was a fucking time piece.

When Murray pulled up I told him he had to vary the time he picked me up.

-I can't, he says, I have to drop the wife off at seven ten, so she can clock in for quarter past, so it's twenty past or you're fucking walking it, Rooftop.

If you think about it, we're all rushing to be at appointed places at appointed times. The net result -

your date with death, and don't be late.

Our Eammon became a Buddhist after me dad died; he believes if you live a good life in this world you get a better one in the next. All I can say is that if I don't pull me socks up, I'll be coming back as a fucking mechanic or worse still a Scouse mechanic .

Anyway, I'm in the cubicle trying the pants on - not a bad fit! If we can't do the Swopsie they'll do for wearing at Belle Vue dogs next Saturday. I change back, come out and notice there's one or two in the shop now. I walk over to Janine, pass her the card, write out the cheque from memory, and I get the fucker perfect! I'm on a roll. She's checking fuck all. She bags the pants and gives me a receipt and me card.

I smile and point to her name above her tit and say,

-What's the other one called?

She smiles.

I nod over at the old cow who's serving some deaf pensioner and making a right fucking meal out of it.

-She looks a right stuck-up bitch, I say.

The smile fades and she says,

-That's my mum.

I pick me bag up and fuck off for a drink.

I head straight back for the pub, some stupid name it had, the Rat and Parrot or something.

Clarissa and Robbie are sat at a table in an alcove right beneath the jukebox speakers. It's playing Billy Joel's *Innocent Man* - not many where I come from, I think. I'm high as a Kiter and want to tell them a ball by ball account of my mission behind enemy lines - Fuck me, says Robbie as I walk through the door, I thought you'd fell off Wigan fucking Pier. Where'd you do?

-B.H.S. - Forty nine ninety eight, I say, chuffed.

I wait for a bit of appreciation but there's more chance of seeing a Mexican Wave at a funeral.

-You've been gone an hour. You could've done four,

he says.

I realise me artistry ain't gonna be appreciated. Never mind, I think, Van Gogh sold fuck all while he was alive, so I just pick up me pint and shut up.

Clarissa sips her Coke, pulls on her jacket and is up ready to go. Nerves of fucking steel the girl's got.

As she leaves I shout,

-Singh as you go, and let the world go by!

I get one good gulp of me beer down, wind Robbie up about Janine in the shop. I've told him that she wants to meet me after work and that she's got the best pair of tits I've ever seen, and Clarissa's back.

Fifteen minutes she's been fucking gone, she must've fucking ran.

I'm gutted. I've had no time to relax.

-Where'd you do ? I say,

-Same as you, she says, beat you by a penny - mine's forty nine ninety nine.

-A penny and three quarters of a fucking hour, Robbie says.

They both look at me. I've still got half a pint in me hand.

-Give us a fucking break, I say; even a Blackpool fucking donkey gets half an hour for its dinner.

Like I say, she was a natural.

One time in Middleton she's Kiting with Scots John and they're in Tesco, and they fill the trolley with fifty quids worth of shopping. When they get to the checkout they're just like any other father and daughter. Clarissa hands over the cheque and card. The girl don't seem happy with the signature so she rings for assistance. Scots John hears a smoke alarm going off in his head and decides to get away from the fire before he's burnt. He looks at Clarissa and says,

-I'll just see how your Mother's getting on, and he walks out and leaves her.

The Supervisor turns up, checks the card against the

list and says there's no problem. She loads the shopping into bags and walks out as cool as you fucking like.

That's how I got taken into the Kiting gang - after that, Scots John was about as popular as Yasser Arafat at a Barmitzvah.

Margery and Clarissa were best mates; them two and Clarissa's sister, Sharon had knocked about together since they were kids. When I first started taking Margery out, Clarissa fell out with Margery because she was spending all her time with me. I remember one time Clarissa shouting up Collyhurst Street,

-You think you're a woman, Margery, you're not; you're just a snotty fucking kid!

I sort of understood that line of thinking. When me mate Dodge first got with Mary it didn't half fuck our partnership up. For years, if one of us had a tenner then both of us had a fiver. Then all of a sudden you're knocking on the door and the cunt can't come out, cos he's baby sitting with some girl.

I can trace the end of mine and Dodge's relationship though to one incident. It was when we robbed Crowthers, with a bad bastard called Bernie Davis. Total unplanned madness it was. We'd been drinking in the Piccadilly Club till about half two in the morning. I was speeded out of me fucking brain. The trouble with that stuff was that it always made me feel like I was a ten year old on his first trip to Blackpool. So the three of us are walking up Oldham Street on our way home. Davis is in a right fucking mood cos he's been buying a right darling double Pernod's all night, and she fucked off while he was at the bar. What's really pissing him off though is that Dodge and me will tell every cunt about it, and Mr Fucking Hardman will look like a mug.

As we cross past Stevenson Square there's this drunk swaying at a bus stop. As we get up to him, Bernie for no apparent reason slaps the poor fucker good and hard. The drunk lets us get maybe twenty yards past him then shouts,

-No fucking need, you tosser.

Talk about Death Wish.

It was bad what happened next; this poor twat is just out for a night on the piss, then fuck off home to his wife. Bernie walks back - as he's walking he's saying,

-You want a fucking fight? I've sunk that fucking low that pieces of shit like you think they can wipe their feet in my fucking face?

Davis gets up to the man, then bang, bang, bang. He's punching the poor cunt stupid. The thing is, he's trapped the twat in a sort of triangle in the shelter and he can't fall. Bernie's punches are holding him up. In the end he just sort of slithers down the shelter, totally fucked.

Davis, the piece of dirt, pulls his prick out and pisses over the drunk's bleeding face and says,

-RIP. Rest In Piss.

Then he walks back to us. Me and Dodge are laughing - we couldn't do fuck all else, there was plenty of room in the bus shelter for two more.

The thing with Davis was, he was a fully trained Mechanic - and I don't mean the sort that fucks around with vehicles. He was a certifiable madman from Cardiff who didn't mind the odds against him. As hard as a Rubik Cube to a blind man. I was in the Heywood on a Monday a couple of months before, having a pint, when this stranger walks in. He was a big lad, looked like he could handle himself. He buys a pint and sits down in Davis's chair by the corner of the bar. No fucking hassle, Davis ain't in. Ten minutes later Bernie enters and he seems in a good mood. He orders a pint shouts over to the man,

-You're in my chair, pal!

The stranger looks around at all the empty chairs

and then at Davis, who is smaller than him, and makes a serious miscalculation. Instead of apologising for everything from the Reichstag Fire, up to and including United's last home defeat, he shouts back,

-I don't see no reserved signs.

Now, he probably thought he'd made an innocent remark, but translated to Welsh what he'd just said was,

-Your Mother sucks off Scousers and your Father takes it up the arse from a Greek.

To put it blunt, Davis murdered him. The first punch took Mr Stranger right off the chair and the second punch took him right off Planet Earth. Then Davis picks up the prized chair that the man thinks is worth a hospital visit for and says,

-You want the fucker, fucking have it, and batters the unconscious figure with it.

The only person with the guts to say anything was this old Desert Rat, Tommy - he just looked at Bernie and said 'Enough'. Bernie looks at him and nods.

When that poor sod next blew his nose I bet he had to look in the mirror for directions.

Anyway, me, Dodge and Bernie walk away from the battered drunk (make a good name for a pub that) and we're up past Crowther's Clothes shop. I'm high, and without any warning I kick the door in. The alarm is going like fuck; we bail in, grab an arm full of leathers each and we're out within minutes. We hit the top of Oldham Street, no Dirty in sight, so we cut across Great Ancoats Street and down by the back of the Daily Express. There's lots of little side streets down there. Years ago when I was a kid it was known as Little Italy. It ain't changed a lot, still full of mills and factories. Anyway we bang all the coats in a skip at the back of a sort of croft thing. It's Saturday night so no problem with workmen early tomorrow. Then we split three different ways, arranging to be at Bernie's house, eight in the morning, with Scots John's van. I do a decent trot cos I know where Dodge is gonna come out, near Granellis, and I want to make sure I'm there before him.

So when Dodge comes round the corner by Prussia Park I'm waiting; I say,

-Come on we'll cut back, get the gear, and fuck Davis.

Dodge is having none of it.

-No way, he says, let's come back in the morning in a van, split it three ways with Davis.

-Fuck off, I say, he'll screw us, you know he will. Let's get the gear, bang it in Charlie's, bung him twenty, he'll be sorted - he fucking hates Davis.

Dodge ain't happy,

-Davis will kill us, he says.

-No, we bluff it out; turn up tomorrow in the motor, act as surprised as him, I say. Fuck him anyway, the Welsh bastard - all they're fit for is getting coal up and burning down holiday homes.

Anyway, I convince Dodge to go back with me. We nip to Charlie's to make sure everything is all right. He says yeah, as long as he never knew where the gear came from. About twenty minutes later we're walking back to Charlie's with our second load of coats, - there were too many for one trip - when it comes on top. Klingons on the starboard bow. The Dirty are everywhere. We drop the coats and run. Like I've already said, I can shift a bit, but Dodge ain't no Linford Christie and he gets rugby tackled and pinned down by the Dirty. I'm up the canal and away.

Net result - because of my stupidity and greed, Dodge gets eight months.

The next morning I carry through the charade with Davis - and when she got there the cupboard was bare. He wants to know where Dodge is. I say I don't know and get a chipped tooth for me trouble. But he seems satisfied that I ain't involved when he hears about

Dodge's arrest, choosing to believe that Dodge was doing the dirty on the pair of us.

Poor Dodge - a term indoors and a hiding from Davis when he comes out.

Anyway back to Clarissa. At the time when my involvement in Kiting began she was living with Robbie in a maisonette off Collyhurst Street, with their first baby Ryan. Robbie wasn't working, just doing a bit of this and that here and there, so he needed quick and easy money just like me.

Robbie got into the Mooching through Bert, who is Clarissa's dad. Bert was Mooching and Kiting before every other cunt jumped on the bandwagon. So Robbie did his YTS with a master, a sort of Obi Wan Kenobi of Kiting. They worked together for about four months, but Bert's style was a bit slow and laid back for Robbie. It was built around the principle of, if the risk ain't worth taking, don't fucking take it. He also favoured a sort of three day week - go out, get enough for a couple of days on the piss in the Vine, then go back out again. Ronnie just wanted to be bang at it.

I liked Bert's sense of humour, it was really cynical, old lag type of stuff like Fletcher in *Porridge*. I was in Robbie's having a can one time when Bert, who's been missing for two weeks and is wanted by the Dirty, comes in.

-Give us a can, he says.

Clarissa, who's been worried to fuck, takes one look at him and says,

-Do you know who's been here for you?

He picks up a can, opens it and says,

-Joan Collins?

Clarissa ignores him totally and says,

-The Police.

He takes a long gulp of the beer and says,

-What, that fucking Sting fella? Well tell him he can fuck his rain forests, I've got enough fucking trouble with me feet.

-Don't you be clever, Clarissa says, D.C. Davey was here before.

-What in a previous existence ? he says, Who the fuck as, King Herod?

And poor Clarissa can't get the cunt to listen or take anything fucking serious.

Well, that's pretty much the history of it.

Funny Red Nose day happens in March. When the one I'm telling you about took place I'd been Kiting for maybe six months, and I'd got the hang of it. But each time Robbie brought a new book to our house to practice, I made him feel about as welcome as a Prodigal Son's return to a Fatted Calf. I was elated by the prospect of easy money, but physically sick with fear. It just wasn't me game.

Anyway, on with the story.

FUNNY RED NOSE DAY

I just knew it was gonna be a twat of a day. Me and Margery were living in a little terraced house in Newton Heath at the time, and we were way behind with the mortgage. I'm drinking like a fish and she's pregnant on the third. I mean, fuck - I'd known the girl forty three months and she'd been pregnant twenty fucking five of them. It had got so I couldn't recognise her without a smock on. It was like I'd spent me whole life changing shitty nappies. I don't mind having the kids, I love each one of them, but they take away your freedom. You start out wondering whether to go and watch Bolton away in London or have a week on the piss, and finish up worrying whether or not you've got enough money for a couple of pairs of kids shoes.

Anyway the day before, me and Robbie had Kited all around Oldham and done in eight cheques. Finished about two-ish. Done the Swopsie with a coat from British Home Stores. Which gave us twenty three quid each. Then we went our separate ways. Robbie with the bags to give to Clarissa to do the Swopsies the same night if possible, or next morning if not. Me on the piss.

So I wake up in the morning on the couch with a storming hangover. I vaguely remember playing three card brag and winning. A fact that's verified by a few crumpled notes on the coffee table. I sit up, me head's spinning. I look round; two or three empty cans and there on the wall unit, the Holy Grail! - about half a bottle of vodka. Now that's what I call a full English fucking Breakfast. I pour meself a vodka and Dandelion and Burdock. What did Ray Milland say in *The Lost Weekend* when he found the booze hid in the lampshade? - *I didn't know I was a Capitalist.*

Then all of a sudden she's in the room.

-That's the kids' mineral you're drinking, she's fucking moaning.

-Get off me back will you, I don't do weightlifting, I say.

It's a mistake. She's ready for an argument and me head feels like Ian Paisley has moved in with a fucking marching band. Every word she speaks is like a fucking thunderclap.

-What fucking time did you fucking come in last night? she's saying.

I'm thinking, what a stupid fucking question. Only one of us knows the answer to that and it ain't me. I say,

-You can't say 'fucking' twice in the same sentence, it constitutes a double fucking negative.

-Don't think you're going out today, she says.

I sit back and let her tidal wave of anger subside.

-I've got to, I say, I'm doing the business with your Robbie.

She gets the fucking Hoover out. The only time she Hoovers is when I've got an hangover or when there's football on the telly. That's it though, no more shouting. I get the deaf and dumb breakfast treatment instead for half an hour. I can hack that. I know the softening of her attitude is due to the fact Robbie's due and he'll have the readies from the Oldham Swopsies. Which means I'll have not far short of two ton, and that she'll be able to screw me for half of it.

She's sat smoking, and staring into space - she should get a job at Jodrell Bank, they'd pay her for it.

Robbie's late.

-Make a cuppa, she says, more of a threat than a request, and I know that the misdemeanours of the night before are about as fucking relevant as the sinking of the Lusitania.

It reminds me of something me Dad once said,

-Whatever state you come home in, always memorise what she made you for tea. Then the next day when things have calmed down a bit, say - that

69

was a nice bit of liver you gave me last night. They start thinking you couldn't have been as drunk as they thought if you can remember what you ate the night before. It worked like a dream for a while, then one day I wake up in me own spew. I get up, clean meself down. Margery's on the couch watching some silly fucking game show, the kid on her knee screaming his head off. So I say,

- Lovely bit of fish last night; want a brew?

-Lovely fish, she says, how the fuck would you know? You spilt it over the fucking baby, you fucking arsehole!

It sort of blew the game after that.

It's gone nine and still no fucking sign of Robbie. I start to brew up for Margery, who's explaining that we need a new cot. I'm thinking fuck the Kiting - if Robbie ain't shown by ten then I've got about eleven quid plus the vodka, and I'm off on the piss.

Margery asks if I've rang in work yet, in a pleasant voice - she's definitely after a new cot out of the Kiting money.

-I rang in yesterday. Told them I had the shits, said I'd be in today if all went well. So fuck 'em, they can expect me when they see me. The way I feel it could develop into Lancashire's first case of Beri-Beri, I shout through.

Even though she's seven months pregnant and I've got a bastard of a hangover I'm weighing up this short tee-shirt thing she's wearing. I slide over next to her on the couch.

-Robbie's got about a hundred and seventy of mine on him, you can have a ton for a cot, I'm saying. As I do so my hands are sliding up her tee-shirt,

-I'd give you more, I say, but I owe fat George fifty.

Me hands are rampant now.

-Let me put Brendan down, she says.

And the next minute we're rolling on the bed. I'm just about to play hide the sausage, when the door knocker goes.

-Ignore it, I say.

-Fuck off she says, Robbie's got the money for you. It'll be him.

Net result - no shag; and I've promised her a fucking ton.

The way Robbie knocks on the door is a bastard. One loud bang followed immediately by twenty louder ones. It's as if he's being chased by a fucking lion and his rifle's jammed. It drives you right up the fucking wall.

I answer the door, then I know it is going to be a twat of a day. The cunt ain't done the Swopsies - he's stood there with the seven fucking bags in his hands.

It pisses me right off.

-You fucking bastard, I say; It's nearly ten - you were supposed to get rid of that stuff yesterday and be here for half fucking eight.

He's giving me a big gap tooth smile, and I know that he's hammered on the weed. So he's gonna make Rip Van fucking Winkle look hyperactive.

-Aw fuck, I say.

He laughs and says,

-Stop fucking worrying Rooftop, I'll burn this lot off in half an hour once I get going.

He walks in, nods to his sister, looks at me and says,

-I could murder a brew; is it OK if I skin up?

He shuffles passed me like Zola Budd on prozac.

-Didn't get a chance to do the Swopsies yesterday. Ryan was bad so I had to wait in for the Doctor.

I take a good look at the cunt. He's an advert for last up worst dressed. Not so much man at C&A as man at fucking Oxfam.

He's got a leather jacket on that went out of fashion with flares, a torn City shirt, a dirty pair of snide wranglers and as Judith Chalmers might say 'he completes his ensemble with a pair of well worn Adidas trainers circa Korean war'.

-Glad to see you made the effort, I say, Clarissa hid the fucking iron again or wot?

-Fuck off, he says and sprawls himself across the settee like he's just finished carrying Sir Edmund's tent up Everest sans oxygen mask.

I go in the kitchen and start to brew up. I can hear them in the living room having a chat about fuck all. Mind you, Margery can keep a fucking wrong number on the phone for forty minutes. Margery says,

-What you got in the bags, anything good?

And I hear her going through the stuff. Robbie's letting her, which means she's gonna find something she wants and it comes out of my fucking half; no skin off Robbie's nose, one less fucking bag to take back.

-Yeah, I hear Robbie saying, It looks great.

But I'm in like a shot and say,

-Don't get attached to nothing, we need the money for a cot.

Her face is screwed up but she can't say nothing cos she ain't got no argument.

-Where's the milk? I say.

-Doorstep, she says.

No cunt makes a move so I go out for it. There's about half a dozen bottles in a crate. I pick up a couple and go back in. As I pass her she says,

-Did he only deliver two?

-No, I reply, but not being a Trilgon from the Planet Frid I've only got the two fucking hands. Robbie sniggers.

-I can carry six, she says,

I don't reply but I'm thinking,

-Yeah, one in each hand and four in your fucking mouth, girl.

I finish making the brew, hand out the cups of tea, and I sit on the couch with a vodka and Dandelion and Burdock. Actually, it ain't as bad as it sounds. I might have invented a new drink, they could call it a VD for short. Robbie lights up his ganja and we're both getting our different fixes.

I sit back, caress me vodka; I'm looking at the wallpaper; it's only been up six month and already it's full of shit. Then I think of the Nurse's uniform and I cheer meself up a bit.

About six month before, I'd been having a Sunday dinner pint with a mate of mine, Jimmy Robbins, when Jim says,

-Look at this! and shows me an advert for a kinky Nurse's outfit.

I'm staring at this skimpily dressed model with this little silk uniform and white bib and hat on.

-What sort of pervert would send for this? he says.

-Give us the fucking advert! I say.

Jimmy gives it to me; I fill it out and put it in me pocket. I get home and I send the fucker off. When it arrives I convince Margery to play Nurse Edith Cavell (before she got shot) - all's well and we have a bit of fun.

I'm back in the Railway a fortnight later having a pint with Jimmy, and the subject of the uniform comes up again. So Jimmy asks,

-Did you ever send for that one the other week?

-Yeah, I say, got the fucker in the house - she wears the lot, even the frilly little bonnet.

So all the darts lads are listening and we have a bit of banter about it, and the subject ends.

Anyway, Tuesday night is darts night and all the boys are there. I can sense an atmosphere, there's a wind-up going on but I can't get to the fucking bottom of it. I'm trying to suss out what this bunch of cunts are up to but they ain't gonna let me in on it. So I think fuck 'em.

The darts end and there's after time, but I can't be bothered cos the shower of twats have pissed me off. I leave about half twelve and when I get to our street I'm surprised to still see the light on.

I wonder what the fuck's going on? She's at me the second I walk through the door.

-You told them didn't you? You said you wouldn't and you have, she says.

I'm well fucking lost - ain't got a fucking clue what she's on about.

-Told who what? I say.

And she's aiming blows at me

-Told them wankers in the pub about the Nurse's uniform! Didn't you?

-Did I fuck, I say, what goes on in our own bedroom is our own business.

I drop my guard as I see her thinking, and she smacks me one right in the eye.

-You lying fucking pig! she says, I've had fourteen fucking calls tonight asking for Nurse fucking Margery!

I'm reeling back, me eye throbbing, thinking I need a new set of mates and a place in a battered husbands' home.

I'm sat there smiling to meself at that devious bastard Jimmy and how he set me up. Robbie's staring at me,

-You drunk? he asks.

-Am I fuck, I say, I'm just reliving the good times, and I empty the remainder of the drink down me throat, stare at a picture of the kids on the wall, and think - who the fuck needs it?

-You believe in all that shite Rooftop? he says.

And for a second I think he means family values but he's pointing to a crucifix next to the kids picture.

-Don't know, I say, Me Mam gave it me. So I put it there to please her. It don't do no harm.

-It's a load of bollocks, Robbie says and there's genuine venom in his voice.

-I used to believe it all, he says, I even used to pray.

As he says this he puts his hands together and lowers

his head. He looks almost angelic in an Angels with dirty faces sort of way.

-You know what stopped me believing? A fucking Priest that's fucking what.

I'm thinking that maybe the Priest had a fucking point. I mean he's no advert for Christianity is he? Not so much the thief that repenteth as the thief who's still bang at it.

-Yeah, dirty bastard, he continues, I helped him say Mass in Borstal. Then he takes me to this room behind the altar. Sits me down and he gets a bottle of wine out. I'm thinking 'Body of Christ' as he pours us a mug full each. I even remember what cup he gave it me in, it had Hull Kingston Rovers on it, rugby or something. I've hated the bastards ever since. Anyway I'm swigging it back thinking not bad this altar boy game, when all of a sudden his hand shoots up me cassock and grabs me knob.

At this point me and Margery collapse into each other laughing. I mean Robbie in a cassock -no way.

-It ain't fucking funny, he's says embarrassed to fuck.

-What did you do? says Margery trying to keep a straight face.

-I fucking butted him, Robbie replies, the cunt only starts crying and saying 'yes I must be punished, punish me.' Well, says Robbie, I punished his fucking head in. As I walk out he's only shouting 'thank you my son' after me.

-Never went near Mass after that, he concludes. It's just a load of bollocks.

There's a stunned silence. I giggle to meself and say,
-Yeah but do you still do the cross dressing?

Robbie shoots me a look as if to say 'forget it or you might get punished'.

And I'm left mulling over the fact that Robbie has turned against God and Hull Kingston Rovers just cos of some masochistic dirt track rider in a dog collar and frock.

-Oh well, I shrug, it takes all sorts.

Margery goes upstairs to get dressed. I can hear the two babies waking. Robbie is rolling another weed. So I decide to pour meself another dose of VD. About sixty forty in favour of the vodka - it would be a shame to waste the kid's mineral. I needed it. It might not have been June the twenty first but it was still gonna be a fucking long day.

-Where's Clarissa today? I ask.

-Took Ryan to the Doctors, then her Mam's, he says.

I thought of having something to eat, but I knew I wouldn't be able to keep it down. I fucking hated Kiting and I knew I was in the wrong physical shape for it.

Margery came downstairs in slow motion, wearing a pink smock. God, the girl's slow; I bet when she takes the kids to school they smack her for dawdling. She's got the baby Rory with her.

-Get him dressed, I say, I'll take him with me.

-No fucking chance, says Margery.

I go into the kitchen and I start making the little fella some of this cereal sort of thing that he has. I make extra to put in a plastic container, just in case he gets peckish at the wrong time while we're out.

I knew she'd relent in the end and let me take him, and if she didn't I'd just use it as an excuse to fuck the day off. I'd do the Swopsies, split the earnings with Robbie, and as Marlene used to say- I'd see what the boys in the backroom will have.

-Make me a milky coffee, she orders.

-Yeah me too, Robbie shouts.

So I'm in the kitchen brewing up and she comes in.

-You can take Rory with you if you want. But he's got a bit of a cold, so watch him will you? she says.

I do the coffees, take them through, pick up me vodka and go upstairs for a shit, a shave and a shower.

The thing about Kiting is you've got to look and feel

76

inconspicuous. I pick out a casual shirt, a pair of trousers and me black leather, and down the vodka.

I go about the business of getting ready, stare at me face in the mirror as I shave. God, how did I get so old so soon? and I think about our Eammon who's older than me, but looks a good couple of years younger and I think, now there's an advert for an honest fucking life.

I can hear Rory crying downstairs and he sounds about as keen as me to do a day's work. I finish off shaving, have a quick shower and take me clothes downstairs for ironing.

I walk into the living room and she's rocking the baby to sleep - a real picture of maternal love, and I think that if she went to a mind reader he'd charge her half price for being with a bastard like me.

I've took a bit of stick off people for using me kids when I go out on little Earners. But the way I look at it is, we're a team and if by having them with me it helps me, then in the long run it helps us all.

Me Dad had a saying when we were kids. It was,

-When I shut that door to go to work at seven in the morning all my friends are on the inside. Anyone not the other side of that door is the enemy.

Now I've got kids of my own I understand. No one is gonna give you fuck all - you've got to go out and take it.

Rory, though only a baby, was the veteran of a lifetime of crime. From the age he was first able to leave the house I'd used him in different things. His debut was in bent Post Office books. It might sound callous but he was a beautiful baby, and all eyes focused on him and not me.

Robbie was rolling again,

-Have one Rooftop - cool you down, he says.

-Fuck, I say, I'll just finish off me vodka then we can fuck off.

I notice there ain't much left of the half bottle and I make a mental note to ease up. The road to Risley is paved with empty spirit bottles.

-Whatever you say, Robbie mutters.

Margery does the ironing, I dress, and the three musketeers are off and running.

ONLY KIDS

Big Tony I suppose is me oldest mate. We go back a long way. We even went to the same Primary School together. He was present at the famous fight with Roddy McKelvin. He always claims I never won it and that it was a draw, but if he's pushed to give a verdict he gives it Roddy on points. Other times he says Roddy only gave in cos I was bleeding on his crucifix. He only does it cos he thinks it winds me up, and the cunt's right - it does.

The first time I remember seeing Tony, we were little more than seven and we were in the toilets in the school yard. Everyone was lining up to go to Benediction after school. I'd discovered a way out of going; at the last minute before you march to Church, you ask to be excused to nip to the toilet. Always ask a soft touch teacher who hardly knows you. Then when you get there let all the genuine weak bladder bastards do their business. When the toilet's empty, go into a cubicle, get behind the door. In them days they went right to the floor. Hold the door open as flat against you as possible. When the teacher checks to see if the toilets are empty he'll look down to the bottom, see the door open, nobody on the bowl and fuck off. You give it ten minutes then you emerge from the shit house and fuck off home for your ball while all your classmates are giving it 'Mea Maxima Culpa'. Anyway, one day I'm emerging from trap one and out of trap two comes Tony, a little younger than me but a good foot taller.

Net result - a lifelong friendship.

The Big Man loves a drink and he don't care what he has to do to get it. That's one of our common bonds. We used to booze together in the Red Bull when we were still in Secondary School - in fact that's what got Tony expelled.

He was sitting at the back of the class one day with a storming hangover. He was about fourteen at the time, but by far the biggest kid in the year. This teacher is giving us a History lesson. I always found them interesting, Tony always ruined them for every other fucker. Anyway this teacher, Atkins, is going on about the Huguenots or some fucking thing, it might have been Juggernauts for all I remember.

Tony's holding his head, he's had enough, so he says loud enough for the whole class to hear,

-Will you fuck off?

Atkins goes blue in the face. His veins are like bicycle pumps. We all turn to stare at Tony.

Atkins yells,

-What did you say Nicholls?

Tony looks up and repeats it.

Atkins is furious, but he can't do a lot; he's half the fucking size of Tony.

-Get to Mr Jackson and repeat what you've just said to me. There's ladies in this class and they don't deserve the gutter behaviour of animals like you, and never step foot in my class again! Atkins yells. It's quite a good speech, apart from the fact that there aren't any ladies in the class, and Tony not returning ain't gonna deprive Cambridge of no History Don.

Tony gets up and walks out heading for the headmaster Jackson's office. Jackson was a strict disciplinarian, a fucking nutter, and a fanatical Catholic. He once sent for me Dad over our Eammon. When me Dad gets there he thinks Eammon's done something serious. Jackson says to him,

-Your Eammon's a bright lad but he's got some funny ideas about Jesus.

Me Dad looked at him and said,

-So have you, you think he's the son of God.

Thanks Dad - they loved the Raffertys in that school afterwards.

Anyway, by this time Tony is ready to say goodbye to his education, so he walks straight into Jackson's office without knocking. He said later that he was hoping to catch the old cunt stuck up the Secretary.

Jackson looks at him puzzled and says,

-What do you want Nicholls?

Tony looks at him, shrugs and says,

-Mr Atkins has told me to come down here and tell you to fuck off.

There's a silence, then Tony adds,

-He mustn't like you.

They expelled him after that, and Tony was left to get his education from the only place that really counts - the street.

I was left to the mercy of the first master criminal I ever met, Vinny Doherty. Me and Tony met Vinny the first day we started at St Martins. We were hanging round the main gate waiting for the opportunity to pick on someone weaker than us. Which wasn't easy cos we were year one and the new intake.

Anyway, Vinny came walking down Cobbley Street in short pants and carrying a fucking briefcase.

He looked like someone who turns up at a fancy dress ball when it isn't.

He was pure Irish and talked like me Dad did when he got angry. I couldn't understand a fucking word. He was an altar boy at St Chad's and he'd signed the pledge aged ten. Amazing people, Catholic priests; they make children swear never to touch alcohol and yet they swan around half pissed most of the time themselves.

Vinny was very easily led; right up to the point where he started leading. At the beginning it was my little gang. Me, Big Tony, Sellotape, Vinny, Molly and our Paddy. But slowly I felt the power being drained from me. Vinny always had the better ideas.

The final nail in me coffin came one afternoon in school. He comes up to me and Tony and sort of whispers,

-Seven o'clock. I've got a couple of big ones lined up, and don't let any fucker know.

Me and Tony were hoping by big ones he meant his two sisters, who played netball for the school. So seven o'clock comes. As we get there his Mam and two sisters are off out on some woman's vigil at the Church.

-Go in, says his Mother in a booming Irish voice. And Me and Tony go in.

She was a lovely woman, Vinny's mother. I bumped into her years later on Moston Lane and she was crying. So I say,

-What's to do, Mrs Doherty ?

She recognises me immediately and smiles.

-Six lovely grandchildren I have Ronald, and not a one will I live to see make their Holy Communion.

I'm thinking, fuck me the poor woman must have cancer or something. So I say,

-Why, what's wrong Mrs Doherty - can I help?

-Help, she says, nobody can help - they're all Protestants.

It might sound daft but that woman would rather have had cancer than Protestant grandchildren. So I change the subject,

-How's Vinny keeping? I say, knowing he's in Hull nick.

-Him, she says, the Devil's own. Eight years he's doing now. What happened to him? He was such a lovely boy when he played with you, Eammon and Patrick. It was that school that made him the way he is.

Anyway Mrs Doherty motions us in and me and Tony walk into the living room. Vinny's at the table. We're three twelve year olds sat around the table. Vinny turns the radio up so we can't be overheard, and says,

-Who can we trust? I need one for the first job and two for the big one.

Me and Tony are entering into the conspiratorial nature of the occasion. But I'm well pissed off cos I definitely ain't Mr Big anymore.

-What about Sellotape? says Tony.

-Not on the first one, says Vinny. It's got to be an insider, someone who goes to St Martin's.

-Our Paddy, I say.

There's a stunned silence.

-He's only eleven, says Vinny, is he up to it?

I'm getting indignant,

-Course he is, I say, he's me cousin.

-OK says Vinny, us three and Paddy for the Martin's job. The same four and Sellotape for the big one.

Me and Tony's had enough fucking about.

-What is it Vinny? says Tony - rob the Secretary's office?

-No, says Vinny - the Two Hundred Club.

The Two Hundred Club was this weekly draw thing. Each parent paid a pound, to be in by Thursday. A draw was made on the Friday afternoon. Three prizes totalling one hundred and fifty pound, with the remaining fifty going into school funds.

So Thursday was the best day to get it. But how? It was kept in a locked drawer in a teacher called Morris's locked classroom.

Vinny's plan was fucking great. We do it at lunchtime. This seemed impossible at first because all the doors in that part of the school were locked at lunch and guarded by prefects. But the plan was fucking simple. When the art block emptied at twelve and Morris fucked off for his dinner time pint in the Alliance, Big Tony and Vinny were to hide in the toilets, leaving the door to a cubicle slightly ajar, and standing on a bowl. What Paddy and me were to do was to make sure Bozo the prefect wasn't able to make a thorough inspection. When he walks down near the last cubicle, before he can push the door open Paddy grabs me and starts calling me a cunt. We start fighting; Bozo the prefect runs over, grabs the pair of us and kicks our arses out the door. As he's doing so Vinny and Tony are out of the toilets and up the stairs.

The next stage was where Vinny came into his own. When Vinny was explaining the plan, I'd spotted the flaw right away.

-Listen, I said, it can't be done.

-Why ? said Vinny smiling. So I told him.

-Every Thursday we have Morris for Art, eleven while twelve. At twelve the buzzer goes and he lines up in the hallway and locks the door. So we all know the door is locked and if we try kicking it in, it will make a noise and the prefects will come. So how do we get past a locked door? I said.

Vinny, as I'm saying this, is just smiling. I know the cunt's got something up his sleeve.

-It took me a while to think of a way round it, he says. Listen, what would your Dad do on a Saturday night if you hid all his shoelaces?

-Batter fuck out of me and go out in shoes without laces. He wouldn't miss his beer for fuck all, I say.

-Yeah, and Morris is the same; you make it that he can't shut the door for some reason and he'll mess with the fucking lock for five minutes then he'll fuck off for a pint. He's on the same dinner as us; he ain't got no time to wait if he wants his three pints, Vinny says.

I see it all now.

-How do we stop him from locking the door? says Tony.

-Simple, says Vinny smugly and I know I'm definitely no longer gang leader. What we do is - Ron on my signal gets Morris talking. Makes sure his back's to me and he can't see nothing. Then I walk up to the door, slide a mixture of wet putty and glue into the lock. I've tried it and it sets in about five minutes. By the time the buzzer goes it's rock hard. When he lines us up in the hallway be bigger cunts than usual, drive the bastard mad. Then he has two choices - he goes for his beer or he cleans out the lock. I'm betting he goes for a pint.

When he's finished he sits back like Hitler in his

bunker. There's one more unsolved problem and he's waiting for someone to ask, but I ain't gonna make a twat of meself again.

-You're probably wondering, he says, how we break open the drawer without Morris noticing as soon as he comes back?

-Pick the lock, says Tony.

I just shrug.

-No, says Vinny, It's a lot simpler than that.

And he draws us a little picture of a desk and a drawer. Then he explains,

-What we do is knock the back off. If you notice, it drops down about two inches lower than the rest of the drawer. God knows why. They tap off and back on again dead easy, I've tried loads.

Me and Tony's looking at him gob smacked; when's he done all this fucking checking out? I'm thinking he mustn't fucking sleep; no wonder he never does any homework.

He walks over to his Mam's cabinet, opens it up and pulls out a little black and red box. It's identical to the one Morris keeps the Two Hundred Club money in. He shows us the key and says in triumph,

-One key fits all boxes. I ought to know, I tried twenty of the fuckers in Woolworth's on Saturday.

That was it, it went like clockwork. I attract Morris's attention, get him on his favourite subject - Impressionist Painters. Vinny does the lock; while Vinny's doing it Tony does a bit of ad-libbing by looking out the window and whistling. Everybody automatically looks his way. The buzzer sounds, Morris wastes about two minutes on the door, can't lock the fucker. Calls it a draw when we sing, 'Why are we waiting?' and fucks off, hearing the call of the Mild. Me and Paddy start a fight. Get slung out. Tony and Vinny leg it up to the Art room. Me and Paddy run round to the back of the school where the Art Room windows face. First hitch -

85

there's two third year girls sat round there talking; they soon fuck off when Paddy starts asking can he see their tits. Vinny knocks the back off the drawer. Tony's keeping lookout.

Both are wearing gloves as a precaution.

Vinny takes his key out - it fits like one of the gloves he's wearing. Opens the box, takes out all the notes and most of the shrapnel, leaving just a couple of coppers and the members list. He puts the back of the drawer back on. Then he goes to the window, puts the money, the key, the gloves and a large pebble in a football sock. Ties the sock up and slings it out the window to me and Paddy. We whip to our Auntie Teresa's, who lives round the corner, and stash the money in her garden shed. Vinny and Tony hide in a different toilet, wait till the doors have been open about five minutes and the place will be half filled with the arseholes who are there to learn. Then they emerge, blend in with the crowd. Meet Me and Paddy in the yard and give each other the gang's secret signal, arrange to meet later and then we split four different ways. Sweet as a nut.

One thing Vinny couldn't have planned for was Morris covering his own arse. He daren't admit that it went when he fucked off and left the door open. So he said he'd checked the money Friday morning and it was all still there. He was adamant that someone had stolen, copied, then returned his keys. Silly twat might have had a University Degree but he was a light year behind Vinny on the brain front.

That night we meet round at Vinny's. His Mam and sisters are out at Church lighting candles for world peace, and good luck to them. Vinny is Mr Big by this time; it's pointless me even trying to make out it's my gang anymore. He gives us forty five pound each, which back then was a fucking fortune, I'll tell you; I was halfway to buying Bolton a new full-back. He keeps a bit extra, not for himself he says, but because the Big Job has got a bit of expenses.

The Big Job was the beginning of the end for our little gang. Again the planning was meticulous but this time that vital commodity was missing, namely luck. It was another master plan for a twelve year old. It was a wages snatch.

Vinny told us that four weeks before, his Dad had been on the sick and he'd been off school. So Vinny's Dad had given him a note to collect the couple of days that were due to him. He told him, go after ten, the wages will be made up by then. The old man worked at Rowley Brothers, a machine shop on the top floor of a Mill. Vinny collected the wages; said he picked them up from the office, which was at the back, facing the canal.

After he'd given us this background information he did a drawing showing us the impossibility of our task. We were on the top floor at the back, there were six doors between the alarmed entrance and the filing cabinet where the wages were kept. Two of these doors were definitely always locked, the other four probably.

After the success of the Two Hundred Club job nobody dared interrupt Vinny, cos we'd sussed out that the cunt would have an answer for any minor road block we could think of.

Then without explaining anything he went on to discuss the perfect time to strike. They got paid anytime between eight and ten on Friday morning, so it had to be before eight. The time they were paid was crucial, it meant one of two things he said. One, the wages were made up on a Thursday night and left in the filing cabinet overnight, or two, they were brought in on Friday morning by Mr Rosenfield who ran the place. Now I'm beginning to think its gonna be a straight forward snatch and grab, so I say,

-He's bound to do them at home and bring them in

Friday morning.

Vinny starts to shake his head then he says,

-I thought that at first, then I got to thinking if that's so, why doesn't he have a set time for paying? I mean, if they're all in a bag why not call everyone in and do it at nine or whatever? So I say to me dad when he's reading the *Universe*, dead innocent like,

- Da, next time I go for your wages, can I go at half eight and then I won't have to queue? Me Da says I'd be waiting a long time cos they might not be ready - Mr Rosenfield makes them up in his office when he gets there.

Paddy, who's following the story like a lurcher follows a fucking rabbit says,

-Yeah but he might be lazy - loads of times I get homework, take it home not done, bring it back not done, and then I do it in school.

There's a look of respect on Vinny's face and I'm beginning to think Paddy's gonna get the number two vote. The way things are going I'll soon figure below fucking Sellotape in this gang.

-I thought of that too, says Vinny, so the last three Friday mornings I've watched him arrive and he gets out of the car with nothing but a fuck off big pink paper.

To me, all Vinny had succeeded to do was make it all impossible. Sure he knew where a load of fucking money was kept overnight, but then again so did I - Barclays fucking Bank. I mean, how were we supposed to kick in between two and six steel doors, go up about twenty flights of stairs, get into the office, break into a filing cabinet and get back out again before the Dirty made the mile round trip from Willert Street Station and arrested us?

Then he unveiled his plan. Again it was fucking simple! All of us he said, had played on the Mill roof often enough. We'd smashed skylights, played hide and seek up there, ripped off anything worth weighing in -

why hadn't the alarms gone off? Fucking simple; the tight fisted bastards had only alarmed the bottom two floors. With Spiderman not being a Miles Platting lad they hadn't thought it necessary to alarm the top two thirds of the Mill, and we were gonna make them pay for it.

So, what we were to do was go up the fire escape onto the mill roof. Four of us tie a rope around a fifth member. Secure the rope to one of the big bollard things up there, wind it round the big pipes, and lower a fifth member down till he's level with the window. He kicks the window in. Climbs in through it. Breaks open the cabinet. Puts the money in a bag. Zips it inside his jacket and we haul him back up.

Vinny told us a week's wages in there was well over two grand. Now he said, we had two problems; one big and one little. The little one he said was finding Sellotape, and the big one was persuading him to let us lower him over a Mill roof into one hundred foot of darkness in the middle of November.

This thought broke us all up, the thought of poor old Sellotape dangling in mid air, his life at our mercy.

I knew Sellotape wouldn't have the bottle to refuse. You find that in life it's the real brave men that tell you to fuck off. The others don't want to look like shit houses so they agree to what fucking ever. Sellotape shit himself but he agreed to do it. With one reservation, he said,

-No way am I undoing the fucking rope at any time. If you want that fucking money it comes up with me, or it stays down there with me.

So there we were on the night, the Famous Five up on the roof. We tie a tow rope to a stump, wrap it round a vent pipe about ten times, tie it to Sellotape. Then the hard bit - getting Sellotape to actually let us lower him. Give the cunt his due, he's got more bottle than me. After about ten minutes he finally sits on the edge, turns round and starts abseiling. Big Tony's our anchor man and we hold on like fuck in front of him. But it's easy enough. Sellotape kicks at the window and there's no real resistance, it shatters in, hardly any noise. Sellotape's getting braver now. He gets on the ledge, puts his hand in and undoes the window, just the one catch like Vinny said, and he's in. Here's where the silly four eyed cunt blew the plan. He can't find the filing cabinet so he turns a light on. Vinny had said no lights, not even a torch. He finds the cabinet, breaks it open with a screwdriver. He's stuffing the money in his jacket when we hear the sirens. The light in the Mill at that height at that time of night had shone like an Old Trafford fucking floodlight, and some twat had phoned the Dirties.

We all look at each other. Nothing is said, but we know we have to haul Sellotape up - can't leave the cunt, much as we'd like to. Now we're tear arsing down fire escapes and along canals. The Dirty are everywhere. It's dark. We've lost track of each other, gone different ways. I can make out our Paddy in front of me, he's crossing a lock to get to the Holland Street side of the canal. I follow the same route. The Dirty are right behind but no way are they gonna risk their lives crossing a lock at night.

Me and Paddy get to Vinny's - no sign of him. I tell Paddy to wait in the opening opposite, keep out of sight while I double back to Tony's, see if he's got away. When I get to Tony's he's on the corner, piss wet through. The mad bastard had jumped in the canal. Fuck that I thought, I'd rather be arrested. To be honest I was more worried about Sellotape, he had the fucking money! Tony said he'd been behind them and they'd jumped into the cellars under the Mill. If they had, I thought they must be caught cos there's no way out of there. Just rats and shit. So much for Vinny, the Brain of fucking Britain.

We found what happened to them a couple of days later. Me and Tony went round to Vinny's house. His sister Bernadette let us in. His face was black and fucking blue.

-God Vinny, I say, did the Dirty do that to you?

-No, he says ashamed, it was me Mam when she got me home.

What had happened was, Vinny had followed Sellotape - he didn't want the money getting caught. Sellotape had ducked into the cellars. Vinny assumed he knew some way out. They drop ten foot into a cellar full of shit, nearly drown, then it dawns on Vinny that Sellotape ain't got a fucking clue where they are. They swim over to a ledge. The Dirty had them cornered. They were shining torches down telling them to come out. Vinny told Sellotape to say fuck all. They hide the money behind a sewage pipe. The Dog handlers turn up, the dogs are going mad to get at them. One of the handlers shouts down,

-Come out now or we send the dogs in.

Vinny said there was no way up, anyway it was a straight fall. Vinny thinks fuck it and shouts back,

-Send in the dogs we'll send them back dead!

He says he could hear the handler throwing a wobbler, telling the Dirty in charge that he wasn't sending his dogs down no rat infested sewer. In the end they lower a ladder and two frogmen come down and take them out, but not before holding their heads under the shit.

The next part of the story really gutted me - the frogmen found the money.

That was it with me and Vinny after that. Him and Sellotape got sent to Rosehill. When they came out Sellotape came back and joined our little gang. Vinny went on to bigger and better things, culminating in fuck off big prison sentences and an article in a Sunday newspaper that called him Mad Dog Doherty.

To think he would have finished up a Catholic priest if he hadn't had met me and Big Tony.

DEAD MOCKINGBIRD

We board the bus to town. I'm carrying Rory and Robbie's carrying the bags. The bus is packed with shoppers; me and Robbie sit opposite each other at the back. I'm travelling backwards. I fucking hate that - I like to know where I'm going, not where I've been. There's hardly any fucking space to move; it's a good job I didn't bring a dead cat cos there's no fucking place to swing it. Robbie puts the bags down and I know what he's gonna do next. He's gonna roll a weed. He's already burnt it at the bus stop. Now he's gonna wind me up by building it on the bus. Not to fucking smoke, cos we're downstairs on a bus and even Robbie ain't that fucking radge. He just wants to see me squirm, rattle me fucking nerves. I'm pretending I don't notice but I'm watching every move the cunt makes.

Rory starts crying for his dummy. I'm searching through me pockets. There's this snooty cow opposite pretending to read but she's secretly wishing it was her stop, and so fucking well was I. I find Rory his dummy, give it him, and he seems happy enough.

Robbie decides to pester the girl.

-What's the book? he says.

-Pardon? she says, like the question has some hidden meaning.

-What you reading? he says, *Fly Fishing* by JR Hartley? And he lifts the book out of her hands.

She's trying not to look flustered but I bet she wishes she'd caught the train to town. I notice the book is *To Kill a Mockingbird* by Harper Lee.

The girl is looking nervous. Robbie looks the book over and passes it back.

-Never heard of it, he says, as if his opinion on literature counts for fuck all.

I have this urge to show this cow that I've read it. Show her that she might think me and Robbie are beneath her, but that we're fucking not. So I say to Robbie, but at her,

-She was a dyke, the woman that wrote that. There's also some dispute if it was her or Truman Capote that actually did the writing.

The girl looks up, unimpressed.

-Does her sexuality really matter? she says, staring me down.

So I stare back, but I don't raise me eyes above her legs. Let's have it right - why does she wear a skirt that short unless she wants men to look at her? I stare long enough to embarrass her, then I say,

-It does if you're stuck in a lift with her, darling.

All conversation ends as we pull up outside New Century Hall. I did me AA stint in there when I came out of Strangeways.

-My name is Ronald Rafferty and I am an Alcoholic.

God, I fucking used to look forward to Alcoholics Anonymous meetings when I was inside. Two free cigs and as much coffee as you could drink. All you had to do was sit back and listen to every fucker's life story. I always invented a different background for meself every week. Told them an alternative history just for amusement. Then this time the screw who ran it, Maloney, says to me,

-Rafferty, why do you change so many of the details from week to week? Is the truth that distressing?

Now this thick Leeds twat thought he had a hold of me Achilles Heel. He thought I was some sort of screwed up fucker with a tormented upbringing. I think the cunt thinks I'm gonna crack up and tell him about some sort of abuse. He's listening intently, but I just smile and say,

-Not distressing boss, just boring, and seeing as you've given up your free time to be here tonight I thought it me duty to try to entertain you.

I'd gone too far; in nick me aim was always to say

nothing and let the others do the talking. If there was gonna be any rooftop protest, despite the nickname, I'd rather be arrested in the basement before things got off the ground. But this time I'd stepped over the invisible line. I'd made a screw look a cunt - and everyone in that room knew it. The golden rule with every screw, no matter how thick they were, and Christ they were thick, always pretend that you thought they had an higher IQ than you. Then wait while they went out of the room and laugh your gonads off at them reading the *Sun*.

Anyway, Maloney looks at me and says,

-You get nowhere in this life being a smart arse, Rafferty.

And a beautiful friendship ended. No more cigs, no more coffee, and I'm kicked off the AA.

I'll tell you something though - eleven years on and Maloney is still a reception screw at Strangeways. So all I'll say is,

-You get nowhere in this life not being a smart arse, Maloney.

The bus drops its load in Piccadilly and we walk down towards Market Street. The girl off the bus is in front of us, walking as fast as her high heels will take her. I'm feeling a bit guilty, not about ruining her day, but I first read *To Kill a Mockingbird* in Detention Centre, and it passed two or three miserable days when I could forget I was stuck with a bunch of sadistic screws and thieving fucking Scousers. So the book to me was like an old friend and it didn't matter a fuck if Harper Lee was gay or not, and all I'll say is if Truman Capote did write it he never reached those heights again. Hey, but who the fuck am I? A fucking book critic?

-Fancy a breakfast, Rooftop? Robbie asks.

-Not really, I say.

Rory's crying and I'm developing a latent fucking hangover. I'm cursing meself for not packing the last drop of vodka in with Rory's bit of grub and bottle.

-Fuck, Rooftop, he says, I'm starving.

-OK, listen, I say, let's do two or three Swopsies, get a bit of work out of the way. Put a few bob in our pockets. Then we'll stop, have a bit of breakfast, and catch the train for Bolton.

Robbie nods,

-Give us a fucking bag, I'll blitz the fucking lot.

And the wheels are in motion.

Whenever I get on a bus it always reminds me of a story a barmaid in the Ram told me years ago. Amy was her name. A belting girl, always served in the vault cos she preferred men's company to women's. You could say what you liked in front of her cos she'd been everywhere and done everything. She was in her forties when she told me the story, but it happened twenty odd years earlier. She was still a fit piece, so you can imagine what she must have been like when she was in her early twenties.

Anyway this day she finishes work in town. It's a lovely summer's night but she's skint and don't fancy the walk. So she thinks fuck it, I'll jump the eighty-two, go upstairs. If the conductor comes up, I'll pretend to be asleep. If he leaves me, well and good; if he wakes me I'll say I left me purse in work, flash me legs a bit and offer him me name and address.

Anyway, the bus comes; she sees the conductor's downstairs. She sees he's about her age, tall and good looking, so she anticipates no problem. She goes upstairs and it's empty. So she sits down on the long seat at the back, and is basically waiting for the bus to get to the Playhouse.

Then she hears steps on the stairs so she assumes her sleeping beauty pose. It's the era of the mini skirt and she's got one on; also because it's a summer's day she's got a skimpy sort of top on.

She hears him approach and cough. But she carries

on pretending. Then he sits down next to her and she can hear him breathing heavy, but she still keeps her eyes shut. Then she feels a hand on her knee. She's thinking, dirty bastard!, but she sort of fancies him so she doesn't mind him having a quick grope for the price of the bus fare. He's happy at first just fondling her knee and she's wondering where the bus is. Then he pushes her legs apart and starts stroking her where it counts. She's getting excited and it's gone too far now for her to open her eyes. Now he's taking proper liberties - he's all over her. He lifts up her top and gets her tits out. She's praying no-one else will come up the stairs.

He's pawing her all over but he's so much better at it than her boyfriend that she just slinks back, eyes closed, and thinks of England. She hears him unzipping and she finds his mutton dagger being put in her hand. She thinks oh well, in for a penny and takes hold of it. His hand's up her skirt and the other's pulling the nipples off her. She's desperate to open her eyes but she thinks it might put him off, and to be fair to him he's giving her as much fun as she's giving him. He's nearly there and he's arched, sucking her right tit for all he's worth. She starts pulling his weapon harder, his right hand is lodged up her skirt.

Then he comes all over her skirt. Dirty bastard, she thinks and opens up her eyes.

It's not the blonde bus conductor. It's some bald man and he's about sixty. She pushes him off. He's thanking her.

-You dirty old bastard! she screams, you've ruined me skirt. He thrusts ten bob in her hand and fucks off downstairs, zipping up.

She's stuck there half undressed, tits bobbing all over the place, trying to sort herself out when the conductor comes up the stairs. He accuses her of being a brass. Then demands the fare. She pays out of the ten bob.

Looks out the window and notices she's miles past her stop. She's half way through Newton Heath.

Like she said, she started out intending to flash her legs at a twenty year old for the price of the bus fare, and ended up giving a sixty year old a wank for ten bob.

-I kept my eyes open after that, she said.

LA RONDE

He was a bad bastard, Bernie Davis. Pure evil. I hated it when he called for me, but I never had the guts to tell him to fuck off. He was the sort of fucking mate that wasn't, if you know what I mean. He was just as likely to smack you as some fucking stranger.

We had a few good earners together and he was useful to have around, because if you crossed someone while earning and he was in your team, it would take a very brave or very fucking stupid man to come after you.

I was with him one time in the Angel on Oldham Road when this woman comes in. She looked the part - smart blue Businesswoman's suit with a matching bag. She walks to the bar and orders a soda water, which in itself was a fucking novelty. I'm surprised the landlord didn't say, - We don't do cocktails.

She asks who the proprietor is, and right away we think it's either the Weights and Measures cos the cunt's watering his beer, or the Social cos his bar staff are signing on and working at the same time.

Both guesses were wrong. She explains that she hires out Karaoke machines and asks One Eye the landlord, if he'd be interested in hiring one. They'd only just come out at the time and only the big pubs in town had them. So really she'd got into the business at the perfect time.

One Eye says he ain't interested; if the shower that drinks in his pub want entertaining they can have a game of darts, or fuck off home.

Anyway, fair play to the girl, she won't be deterred. She says,

-Would you like me to demonstrate for you?

And I'm thinking you could get a fucking hard-on listening to this girl. Then she adds,

-I've three in the van outside, would you like me to

wheel one in for you?

Every ear in the room pricked up, even the old fuckers way past an earner knew the score. You could see pint pots being put down and people sliding out the door. Not many faster than me and Davis.

She's still at the bar and she's still giving it a heavy sales pitch. The silly cow don't realise she no longer has anything to heavy sell. As I'm going out the door she's saying,

-A months free trial - if you can't see the benefit then just return the machine.

When me and Davis get to the van some Juvenile Delinquent is panning the windows with a brick.

There's about twenty Jackals and three fucking Karaokes, but the odds are stacked heavily in my favour cos I'm with the King Jackal, Davis. He pulls a couple of young kids out of the way. They got to learn no one eats till the leader of the pack has finished. I jump in the back, grab hold of the biggest box, a cunt of a thing with JVC on the side. Davis grabs the other end and we start to carry it across Butler Street towards the flats. As it's all going off Mrs Businesswoman comes running out of the pub - she must have heard all the fucking commotion; either that or she got fucking lonely in there on her own. She takes one look at the van and she starts screaming her head off. Not a lot of use round there. Blind Pew saw more than any passer by is willing to admit to. The poor girl's in hysterics. Someone takes her back into the pub. One Eye gives her a brandy and takes his time ringing the Dirty. He doesn't want to get any of his regulars arrested. The magic number nine-nine-nine empties the pub faster than a shout of, 'The beers off!'

She explains to One Eye that she's invested all her redundancy money in the Karaoke business. As she does so Dodge walks in. Me and Davis sent him to try and find out how much what we've got is worth. It makes good fucking sense to find out what something's worth retail before you start trying to flog it.

Dodge listens in for a bit, then he says,

They're complete bastards round here. How much are them things worth?

-About seven hundred and fifty pound each, she says.

-Jesus, says Dodge - it's a good job you're insured.

-I'm not, she says.

And her mascara is running all over her face- *Who's Sorry Now, Whose Heart Is Breaking?*

So she looks for her bag to get a tissue out to wipe away the tears and she discovers that while she's been outside trying to stabilise her little business venture, one of the old fuckers who looked nailed to the wall has relived his youth, and had it away with her bag. What did Jack Nicholson say?

-Never mind, it's just Chinatown.

I'll bet that poor cow never went north of Didsbury again in a fucking hurry.

Me and Davis got two hundred and fifty for it off the landlord of an Irish pub down the bottom of Oldham Road. We had to laugh; the lad we sold it to said,

-It was only this morning I had a bit of skirt in here trying to rent me one.

Me and Davis had a hundred and fifteen a piece and we gave Dodge twenty for a booze. It was Friday night, so we went on a two day bender.

Thing with Davis though is, even when it's a good night you still can't enjoy it cos the cunt never lets you settle. You're always waiting for something to happen or some fucker to get hurt, and you're always praying it ain't you. We were in the Heywood having a game of pool and a crack about the Karaoke. It was now Saturday night and we'd lost a few bob on the horses. Never mind, it was only Mrs Businesswoman's redundancy money. Davis was sat down and Sellotape was going on about education. He was up to his eyes on speed and made up, cos his little brother Superglue had just passed an entrance exam for Manchester Grammar School. He was mouthing it off about Hot House Education, so I said,

-Yeah, that's all right for them rich cunts innit? They identify some smart arse working class kid who's ahead of the field. Take him out and put him in a school full of other smart arse kids. Spend fortunes on the best equipment. Special fucking tutoring, the fucking monty. They pick some kid five furlongs out in front of the field and give him the fucking help to get twenty ahead. Why don't they pick some thick bastard twenty lengths behind the fucking field, spend the same amount of money and get him up there?

The arguments raging now. Sellotape's angry, full of sibling pride. He launches into me,

-You can't say 'well done' to no fucker can you? You've always got to make everything fucking small. Well, you know this fucking Communism you're always fucking spouting? Well if them hypocritical cunts ever got in power, people like you would be the first against the wall. But even then you'd probably be all right, cos cunts like you would have sold the fucking bullets.

The argument's in full swing, both me and Sellotape are enjoying it. The rest of the fucking pub might be pissed off, but fuck them.

Davis has heard enough,

-Are you fucking playing pool or what? he says.

Sellotape sort of waves his hand at him and says,

-In a minute.

I'm too engrossed in me argument with Sellotape to bother about Davis; I've got to show this twat that private education is wrong. So I don't notice when the bastard comes up behind us and smacks our heads together and says,

-Education debate over - you're a pair of thick cunts anyway.

I think, fucking moron, but the thought doesn't develop any further.

We play a bit more pool, have a few more pints and Sellotape fucks off home. He's a bit of an Optician when it comes to drinking- two fucking glasses and he makes a spectacle of himself. What did Dirty Harry say,

-A man gotta know his limitations.

Me and Davis have a bit of after time. I'm ready to fuck off home to Margery when he says,

-Fancy a curry, Rooftop?

-Yeah no problem, I say, thinking he means a carry out from the Wu Fung or a sit in at the Orient Express.

Well fucking wrong on both counts - we're going back to Davis's house for one. I should have realised me mistake right away, but once I'd accepted his invitation it would be suicide to turn it down. Anyway, when we get to his house it's in total darkness and the man of the house ain't got no key. So he starts kicking and banging on the door and I can hear his kids crying upstairs. I've lost all concept of time. I know we had after time so it could be any hour now.

After about ten minutes Davis's wife Audrey comes to the window. She looks down and I might be misreading her look, but I don't think she's expecting company. Talk about 'guess who's coming to fucking dinner?'

Audrey comes downstairs in a nightcoat and answers the door - she's totally pissed off. Me and Audrey go back a bit; she was me cousin Mary's best friend at school, and we all used to play Monopoly together when we were kids. She always used to be the top hat and I was always the dog. I think about mentioning it, but in my drunken state I don't think this is the time or the place. Thank fuck I don't, Davis would think I was inferring something and break me fucking nose.

We're inside the house and it's spotless considering she's got three young kids, and it's a credit to her cos

103

somehow I can't see Bernie behind a Hoover.

-Why didn't you take your keys ? she says, I've only just got me head down.

I look at her and for the first time ever I notice the dark bags beneath her eyes and I'm thinking- Jesus she was the best looking girl in our Paddy's class. I used to spend half me dinner hour watching her play netball and now look at her.

-Don't need no fucking key when I got me Cardiff clog, he says pointing to a size ten boot, opened more doors than a screws pass key this fucker has.

I start to snigger but one sideways glance from Audrey stops me in me tracks.

-Don't be making no noise, she says walking back towards the stairs, the kids have gotta be up early.

It's more a plea than a request and I wish I'd fucked off home with Sellotape.

Then it happens - Davis says,

-Get the chips on doll, and a curry for me and Rooftop.

-Like fuck I will, Audrey says.

And I can see what's coming next. I've got time to get in between, but no such fucking inclination. I once seen this cunt stick a bottle in his brother's face over a game of snooker. So I'm keeping out of it.

He walks over to her, slow and menacing. He's smiling. Then bam, his arm must move but I don't see it. Audrey's reeling back and there's blood pouring from her nose.

He holds her by the shoulders. I'm shaking with fear. He talks to her like he's talking to a naughty puppy,

-Now, while I get *Jim'll Fix It* on the phone for your nose, you go in that kitchen and you make curry, chips and beans for two. Got it, doll?

There's a silence that's impossible to fill. Audrey looks at me and Christ, I wish I didn't know her - that way I could retain some dignity. But I do - and I can't.

Audrey goes into the kitchen to rattle those pots and pans. Davis looks at me as if nothing had happened and says,

-She makes a lovely curry.

Then it dawned on me. Nothing really had happened. In his fucked up world this was his norm.

He walks over to a display cabinet thing, pulls on the pulldown, and it comes off in his hands.

-Don't know me own strength, he says.

And I realise I hate this friend of mine. I also realise for the first time just how frightened I am of him.

He pours two cans of Long Life and we discuss football. About three quarters of an hour later Audrey comes out with the curry, and it looks just how you'd imagine someone with a broken nose would cook for her assailant and his arsehole of an assistant.

-Any bread Rooftop? mein host enquires.

But I say no. I'd hate to see the poor girl humiliated again.

Anyway, I'm on me second Long Life, half way through me curry when I decide I've had enough.

-Cheers Bernie, I say, that was great.

He stops in mid action, a fork halfway to his mouth.

-What? he says, and me blood runs cold. Listen cunty, my wife got up at gone two in the morning to cook that fucking dinner. You eat the fucking dinner or I rub your fucking nose in it, then you fucking eat it.

I have no choice, I carry on eating. It's fucking vile and by now cold, but he will do what he threatens so I force it down. Thank fuck I didn't have any bread.

He looks at the clock and says,

-It's half three - better call it a draw.

It's more a fucking order than an opinion. I say,

-OK if I get me head down on your couch, Bernie?

It's a daft question.

-On your fucking bike; it's not a fucking doss house, and I'm not leaving a thieving little cunt like you down

105

here alone.

Cheers mate I think, and I walk out into a Miles Platting night.

No place to head now but Charlie's. There's no way Margery's gonna let me in, and there's no way I really want to face her. I've fuck all money left worth having, the fucking horses have seen to that, and I've been AWOL for two days. So she ain't gonna be grilling no Fatted Calf. Talk about the Lost Weekend!

I always liked Charlie, even when I was conning and robbing him. He was an ageing homosexual. I don't use that word to put him down, it's just how he considered himself. He wasn't one of these heart on the sleeve arseholes. One time Maurice says to him,

-Hey Charlie, are you gay?

It was a sort of attempted piss take. Charlie laughs and says,

-How can I be? I've got a Doctor's certificate saying I'm a Manic Depressive.

He used to let any fucker stay at his flat as long as you abided by his rules and didn't stay too fucking long. All sorts of people passed through there. The thing I liked about him was he didn't give a fuck about people's sexual preferences. If you weren't his way inclined, no bother - he didn't pester you. When I see all this Equal Opportunities shite I always think about Charlie; he never went around telling every fucker he was their equal and wearing stupid badges. Charlie didn't need to, he thought he was their better. It was at Charlie's that I learnt how to read. Well not so much how to read, but how to love reading. He had boxes of books on all kinds of subjects and when me, Tony and Sellotape fucked off from school we'd sit there reading, and cadging money off the old twat. Me and Sellotape read everything. Tony only read porn, with one notable exception. One day Sellotape picks up 'Fanny by Gaslight' and throws it to him.

-What's it about ? says the big fella.

-Shagging during the Miner's strike, laughs Sellotape.

-I'll give it a go, says Tony.

And before you know it he's twenty pages into the fucker.

-Any good, I say smirking.

-Loada shite, he says- no fucker's shagged no fucker and no cunt's bin near no pit.

We actually improved our knowledge by missing school, cos we learnt fuck all there.

Charlie loved Dickens, and I don't just mean the gay club in town. That's where he got his name from; nobody ever found out his real one. I kicked off reading them to get on the right side of Charlie so I could tap him for some money for cider, but in the end I was hooked.

He was bright as well, Charlie; nobody's mug, a real free thinker, and I don't just mean on sex. I can remember him once explaining to me that the true hero of Oliver Twist was Fagin and not Oliver. He said all these young kids were on the run in London from Workhouses, Prostitution and White Slavers and whatever, and there was no social structure to safeguard their welfare. Yet this fucking social leper, this Jewboy, took them in and supplied them with a home and food. All they had to do was to go out and thieve for him. But if you looked at how he lived, what the fuck did he have to show for it all? Fuck all. He lived in a rat infested shit hole. He was also the only one protecting them from vultures like that twat, Bill Sikes. I told all this to an English teacher at school, but the cunt couldn't take it in. He could only think in straight lines - Charlie could think round corners.

He was a right foul mouthed bastard, Charlie. I think that's where I picked it up. I loved the way he could introduce profanity into any sentence and it sounded like it belonged. Like the sentence would be a wall without cement if he hadn't swore.

-Charlie, one kid says onetime, it shows a lack of vocabulary if you swear.

The arsehole must have picked that sort of shit up from his Mother. There's about six of us listening, so Charlie says,

-Open up the dictionary anywhere, and if I can't tell you what the word means I'll give you a pound.

We're all watching, thinking there's a lot of fucking words in there; he can't know them all.

The kid studies hard, picks one he thinks will fuck Charlie, and says,

-Antediluvian.

I think to meself it's a twat of a word. Charlie milks the silence then says,

-Appertaining to before the Great fucking Flood.

You should've seen the kids face. End of fucking errand. One nil and the cup to Charlie.

Me favourite memory from Charlie's though is of Marie Doyle. I was about thirteen and I'd fucked off from school. Charlie had gone shopping when she turned up. He'd told me to let no-one in, but she was sixteen at the time and she just barged right past me. So she goes in, tells me she's gonna have a bath. She's got a little bag full of clothes with her. I go back into the living room, carry on with me reading. Then ten minutes later and she walks in the room naked. I didn't know where to look or what to do. It was the first time I'd seen a girl in the nude. I just sat there staring at her massive tits. Me face red as a beetroot.

She turns round, sort of smiles and like a fool I look away.

I'll tell you, there's many a day over the years I wish I could have turned the clock back...

Anyway Charlie was a soft touch, so after leaving Bernie Davis's I end up there.

Where Charlie lived is in New Cross, a place called

Victoria Dwellings. They are the oldest purpose-built Council dwellings in Europe - honest, no bullshit. God knows how fucking old. What does Manchester City Council do? Jam the fucking place with pensioners. It's on the edge of town, so any pissed up arsehole from Miles Platting, Ancoats, Monsall or Collyhurst can wander through it after the pubs, pissing against the walls, shagging on the stairs and singing whatever song comes to mind. The Council want to get off their arse and introduce a little bit of Equal Opportunities for old people.

So this day I get there. Charlie lives on the second floor. I walk up the stairs. I'm hoping to Christ he ain't got no special friend there, cos if he has there ain't no fucking chance of getting in. It's late so I've got to knock the deaf old cunt up. I give the door a good clatter. Fuck the neighbours.

-Charlie! I'm shouting through the letter box.

No fucking answer.

-Charlie, it's Rooftop - let me in!

Finally about ten minutes later I hear all these bolts and chains being undone. I think thank fuck for that.

He answers the door, it's fuck knows what time and he's still got his overalls and flat cap on. Mad old twat.

-What do you want, Buster? he says.

He's half pissed. But he's opened the door, and I can tell he's not in a mood cos he called me Buster.

-Just been chased by the Dirty, I lie. Lost them at the back of the Express. Let us in, Chas.

I get in - it's like a fucking oven. There's another guest, a Monsall wanker called Doddy. We ain't no great friends but we nod.

Doddy's got a Newcastle Brown Ale in his hand.

I sit down, say nothing. If Charlie wants me to have a drink he'll offer, and if he don't I won't get a drink, no matter what. I've played these games before.

I listen to the conversation. Doddy's a car thief with

no brains. He has the motors away and his mate Mully rings them. All risk Doddy, all profit Mully. I'm thinking of making the shifty little bastard a mate meself.

-Like I was saying, I've got good probation reports so I might get a suspended, Doddy says.

Charlie's nodding, but I can tell he ain't fucking interested.

The conversation dies and Charlie says,

-Some cans in the bath, cunty.

So I wander into the bathroom. The same bath I should've got in with Marie Doyle all those years ago.

Charlie's got no fridge so he keeps his beer under cold water in the bath. I get meself an India Pale, return to the front room. Monsall's entry for Mastermind is still mouthing off. I grab a chair and decide to get a bit of kip. I pull me coat over me, swig a good gulp of me Pale Ale and get me head down.

I'm just nodding off when I hear Doddy saying,

-We've got a rake full of the stuff in a lock-up near Queens Road - Mully reckons they'll fetch between twenty and thirty each.

Now he's made his fatal mistake. If you know something and someone else don't, then you're winning one nil; don't let the cunts equalise. I ain't got a clue what he's got stashed but I know that Mully's garage is just off Queens Road, and I know exactly where, cos I've sold him wheels and tyres in the past. So whatever is in there now is about to become their ex-property.

The arsehole carries on muttering but nothing else worth hearing comes out. He's the sort of cunt the Dirty have a problem with when they're taking statements. It ain't getting them to talk, it's getting them to shut up once they've fucking started.

The next thing I know it's six thirty. Charlie's waking us up cos he's got work and he ain't gonna leave two thieving toe rags like us to plunder what ever he's got. Me and Doddy hit the street and Charlie bungs us a hand full of shrapnel to get a couple of coffees in Granellis. It's somewhere to go till the world comes alive. We get there just as it's opening. Doddy's got the change so he orders us a coffee each and one bowl of French Onion soup for himself. I ain't hungry; I can still taste the curry from Davis's. If I'd have found out that Audrey had put rat poison in it I wouldn't have blamed her. I'm thinking to meself, I've got to ditch this cunt as soon as possible. Go back, get Davis, get hold of Scots John's van and empty Mully's garage before he opens up at ten. I hate Davis, but at least I've got some back up if half of Monsall's after me. I leave Doddy slurping back his soup and ordering another cob. I'll tell you if the cunt ever wins an around the world cruise there's no way he's gonna be invited to sit at the Captain's table. If this is how he handles a bowl of soup, a full fucking dinner would have to be a designated hard hat area.

I get to Davis's - this I ain't relishing. I bang fuck out of the door and I hear his kids crying. The window opens - it's Audrey. Her face is a mess, and I feel about as welcome as a dingo at a Christening. But she just looks down at me, comes downstairs opens the door; doesn't say a word, and fucks off back upstairs.

So I'm sat on the couch waiting for the Man who shot Liberty Vallance. I survey the room, it's spotless. Fuck me I think, after Davis has gone to bed, Audrey has cleaned up. Get some fucking rat poison girl, a life in nick is at least a life.

Davis comes in. He looks shite; he takes one look at me and says,

-This better be good, wanker.

-I think I've found us a little earner, I say, smiling.

And it's a bit like that fucking French play, La Ronde. The circle starts again. Thieving, drinking, sleeping - thieving, drinking, sleeping - thieving......

I'm sat there while the cunt's getting ready and I'm

thinking - what a fucking life!

HARRY TEACH

Piccadilly's swarming with arseholes. Funny Red Nose Day is in full swing. Grown men are dressed up as St Trinian's schoolgirls. It makes you fucking wonder, don't it? I mean, why don't they just come out of the closet with their mother's best dress on instead of all this fucking pretending? I mean, who the fuck are they kidding, going round making out they're saving the Third World from starvation from inside a basque? It's a complete load of bollocks.

Same as all these charity collectors - what a load of shite that is. I'd like to see how much of that goes to buying Nanook of the North a fucking fishing rod. Years ago when I was a kid, maybe ten or eleven, me and a mate of mine, Jacko, worked for them cunning Bible carrying bastards. They used to pick us up in the morning, give us a box each then we'd do a tour of the pubs rotating our areas. Jacko sang a bit so he'd belt out the *Old Rugged Cross*. While he was doing it me and the God squad used to rattle boxes under people's noses. Talk about a good little Earner. At the end of the night they'd bung me and Jacko a couple of quid each and arrange to meet us the next week. Fuck all went to the old and needy - it was all had by the young and fucking greedy. It all went well till somebody I knew spotted me and told me mam. She soon put a stop to it but, I'm not sure what she objected to most - the thieving from charity boxes or the knocking around with Protestants.

The only good use for a bible I ever found was told to me by an old thief called Harry Teach. I worked with Harry at the Council. He was a driver, though fuck knows how the cunt passed his test.

The thing that I liked about him was his pettiness. At the time he was getting on for about fifty five, but he'd still pinch everything not nailed down. If you put your dinner in your locker and didn't lock it, come twelve o'clock half your butties would be gone.

A lot of the lads got wound up about it, but I knew the cunt meant nowt by it. It was just Harry's nature - Bird got to fly, Wasp got to sting, and Harry got to steal. We had a sort of ritual; I'd find some of me butties gone and half me Kit Kat. So I'd say,

-Harry, why not take the lot?

and he'd smile and say,

-Cos I like you, Rooftop.

Then I'd say,

-Well why don't you pinch Selby's?

And he'd say,

-I can't stand the cunt; and I don't like his fucking scran neither.

Anyway, this kleptomaniac was in charge of a thing called the Milk Run, and his job was to take all the mail to the outlying depots and pick up anything that had to come back. Anything he liked the look of he had away. I'll tell you the shifty little cunt could get where a Benidorm stripper's snake couldn't.

So this day he's delivering mail to Langley; on his way he's dropping me off in Blackley cos I've got a storming hangover, and on the dashboard is a Bible. Now Harry with a Bible is a bit like the Pope with a Playboy, so I say,

-Fuck me Harry, where'd you pinch that from?

-Never pinched it, says Harry - it's mine.

-Fuck off, I say.

He forgets all about the road, picks up the Bible, puts it on the steering wheel, changes hands and swerving all over the road says,

-I, Harry Albert Teach, did not steal this Bible.

I'm gobsmacked; I think I've misjudged the man.

-Sorry H, I say, I didn't know you were into that sort of religious stuff.

-I'm not, says Harry, but I carry one of these where

ever I go. It serves its purpose.

Me head's pounding. I'm willing to let the subject drop, but Harry ain't.

-It has its purpose in nick and it has its purpose out of nick, he says.

He's looking over at me but I'm on the verge of throwing up, and I'd rather he watched the fucking road than me.

-Yeah, he carries on - know what they are?

I shake me head. I've not got the strength to speak and I'm sorry I started this.

-Ever felt the pages? Nice, soft and thin, he says.

The van's careering all over Rochdale Road as he fingers the pages. But he's got me wondering what the fuck he's on about.

-Go on, I say, what the fuck has the feel of the paper got to do with anything?

Harry's laughing and I know the cunt's had me over.

-Well, he says, in nick if you can't get a ciggy paper these are fucking perfect, and plenty of it. You'd be in an Iron Lung four times fucking over before you'd smoked your way halfway through Genesis; and out of nick, if you're ever caught short wanting a shit while you're out in your cab, this stuff is a lot softer than newspaper. So I always keep one handy on me dash.

And he starts laughing; it's infectious, and despite me hangover I find meself rocking and giggling at Harry's use for St Paul to the Corinthians.

He pulls up outside me Mam's and I get out.

-Some butties in me locker if you want them, I say.

-Corn beef, he says - I've already had them. I knew you wouldn't want them, fucking state of you. If you can't take it, don't drink it.

And he fucks off up the road with a honk of the horn and a trail of diesel smoke.

I'll tell you, I've often thought that if a lot more people throughout History would've had Harry's insight for the best use for a Bible there would have been a lot less wars.

Piccadilly is full of life.

-Good day for it, says Robbie.

I know what he means. There's Funny Red Nose fuckers on every corner and they're gonna be that screwed up on their own little ego trips that the shopkeepers aren't even gonna notice two men and a baby.

-First stop for me, I say, is to get me hands on one of them Funny Red Noses.

Robbie laughs and says,

-You don't fucking need one with that boozer's snout of yours.

I laugh - and maybe it ain't gonna be a twat of a day after all.

SELLOTAPE

Some people never get an even bounce of the ball. Sellotape was one. God, that fucker was jinxed. If anything could go wrong in his life, then it fucking went wrong. One of the reasons I hope there's no such thing as reincarnation is that I might come back as that un-lucky fucker. I'll tell you compared to him the Ancient Mariner was a lottery winner. I was playing pool with him one day in the Ram, and Paddy Leary comes in. Now the thing about Paddy is that his Mam and Dad were travellers who had settled in Manchester, but when they first came here they lived on a croft in a caravan. His Dad did odd jobs and a bit of carpentry, and his Mam went door to door selling lucky heather and pegs. So as a result, Paddy was a primed bomb and touchy as fuck about his parentage. Anyway, this day he's been to a funeral or something and he's got his best suit on. Sellotape, wanting to be friendly, lets on. Paddy's in a good enough mood. Then Sellotape says,

-That's a nice suit Paddy - did you get it off the peg?

I swear it was an innocent remark. But to Paddy he was being made a cunt of and he'd just had his parents insulted by a grinning, four-eyed fucking Englishman. Paddy didn't say a word; he just walked round the table and starts raining blows in at poor old Sellotape.

Sellotape crumples to the floor, still none the wiser about what the fuck he'd done.

I'm on the other side of the pool table saying,

-He didn't mean nothing Paddy. Leave it, sham.

And Paddy's off it, screaming,

-You bunch of hounds bastards, ye! I'll kill the fucking lot of you I will!

Like I say, the twat was cursed with bad luck.

The girl he married, Denise Warren, her nickname was Bunny, and it had fuck all to do with her surname and the habitat of rabbits. She was one of the Canal

Girls. These were a bunch of girls who lived down near the Canal and hung around there after school. The idea was to ambush them by the bridge where they hung out and give them the choice - either they consented to some form of sex or they went for a swim. It was a sort of game; they knew we were gonna turn up every night, so if they weren't interested why'd they wait to be chased? It was a sort of mating ritual. The old joke about Bunny was that after being caught a couple of hundred times she still hadn't got her feet wet.

She was always chewing gum and winding it and boys round her little finger. She loved making dirty remarks and embarrassing you.

I remember once, there was about four of us and about six of the Canal Girls, so we gave chase. I caught Bunny right away. I say caught, looking back it wasn't much of a chase. So I get her under this bridge at Butler Street. She stands there panting against a wall. She hadn't done much fucking running so I can only assume that she suffered from asthma. Most of the girls when you caught them used to let you grope them.

So I start mauling her tits for all they're worth. She had a fair pair on her. She sort of leans back, chewing gum, and says,

-Are you gonna do it then?

I get her against the underside of the bridge. I'm eager as fuck, and it's all over before it's started, and I do mean all over. There's a look of disgust in her eyes.

-Fuck me, she says, is that it?

I'm certain she expected me to bring her to the dizzy heights of sexual fulfilment on a canal bank at ten o'clock at night in the middle of fucking November.

-Yeah, I say, when I'm on form I can come even faster than that.

And I walk away, leaving her pulling her knickers up and threatening to tell her Dad what I'd done. A fucking lot that old piss head would've cared.

She always made sure she outran me after that, though she managed to get caught by plenty of others.

Funny thing about Sellotape - despite it all, he married her. She came to him one day, told him that she was pregnant and that it was his, and he did the honourable thing. Stupid bastard.

Dodge suggested we put a name card round, a pound a piece, the winner gets forty pound to buy a marriage certificate and the hand of Bunny in Holy Matrimony. I said what's the point? Sellotape might as well keep his pound cos with his luck he'd win the card anyway. We left her alone after that, despite it always being put on a plate. I mean, let's have it right, a friend is a fucking friend.

Sellotape's whole family had nicknames. His Dad was known as Permanently cos he was never sober, and his Mam, who also declined to abjure the grape, went by the non-de-plume of Sozzled. His younger brother, whose real name escapes me, had the same deficiency on the optical front as Sellotape and was called Superglue - due to the fact that he wore glasses without Sellotape, so everyone reckoned that he'd superglued them together. It just shows that you can't win with smart arses.

Sozzled was a funny woman. For the first twenty years or so that I knew her she lived in a maisonette opposite us and we never saw her sober. The only one who didn't call her Sozzled, apart from her immediate family, was me Dad - he insisted on saying,

-Morning Mrs Reilly. It would be a grand day to wake in Galway to.

She seemed to wear the same clothes all that twenty years, even to Mass on a Sunday morning. Then an amazing thing happened - she became a Jehovah's Witness. A sort of overnight conversion. She bought a day return to Damascus. She was suddenly sober, a state of affairs that embarrassed the whole fucking neighbourhood. People who'd ignored her suddenly weren't allowed to; she'd cross the street to pass on God's good news. She became active on the Council, fighting for everything from children's playgrounds to half way houses for alcoholics. People who had talked down to her were shocked to find she was actually twice as bright as them. Those who had pitied her were now the subject of her pity. In short, she became that fucking nice that everyone hated the fucking sight of her. Apart from me Dad, who didn't seem to notice; he just went right on saying,

-Morning Mrs Reilly. Sure it would be a lovely morning to wake in Galway to.

To poor old Sellotape, it was another nail in the sad twat's coffin. I remember him saying,

-With my family it's like being an Ice Cream girl at the fucking Playhouse picture house. There's a great big beam of fucking light surrounding you, and every cunt's staring at you.

I never made me mind up whether I liked her better as Sozzled, or a fucking soothsayer. She gave me a card once that read,

-Mark, 8:36.

So I said,

-I'm sorry Mrs Reilly, but I don't back dogs anymore. She just smiled and asked me to keep the card.

About twenty years later when Mrs Reilly had gone mad and Permanently had died of drink related causes, and Superglue had become a Doctor and Sellotape had fucked off to Lindisfarne selling mead or what fucking ever, I walked past a church near Albert Square and there was one of them stupid fucking messages outside. It read:

What profit a man if he gain the whole world
yet lose his own soul ?
Mark, 8:36.

It took me out of me stride a bit. I just stood there

staring at it as people drifted by, and I couldn't help but think,

-It would be a fine morning to wake in Galway to.

I was supposed to be on some Health and Safety course at the Town Hall, but after reading that I fucked off into Central Library, grabbed a book, and waited till the pubs opened.

Permanently was a funny fucker - he spoke in riddles. None of us kids could understand a fucking word he was fucking saying. It wasn't just that he was always drunk, cos most of our Dads drank. It was just he sort of said things different. Me Dad said he was the cleverest man he knew, but me Dad was a labourer on a building site, so his opinion didn't really count for a lot.

He'd worked as a manager in a big joinery firm and got caught up in an Earner. When it came on top he got three years. Not cos he was the Mr Big but because he was the most senior man involved, and the Judge accused him of abusing a position of trust. When he came out the only work he could find was as a cleaner on British Rail. I think the humiliation was what drove him to the drink. He was a fucking good carpenter though, he made me a rabbit hutch for me tenth birthday. A fucking belter it was, but typical of the gibberish he talked, he asked me not to keep rabbits in it because, 'Bars a prison do make'.

Yeah, he fucked off to Lindisfarne, Sellotape did, never to be seen again. Except for one fucking letter he sent to Big Tony. The bastard blamed me for every injustice from the Peterloo Massacre to the Maxwell Pension Fund Fraud. He seemed to think that I'd dedicated me life to making his life a fucking misery. It made Norma Desmond in *Sunset Boulevard* look well adjusted.

What started the cunt's fucking gripe was we got arrested together for robbing a bookmakers, and instead of being dealt with at the Magistrates I elected to go to the Crown. The pretext that I used was that I was gonna plead not guilty, when I knew that come the glorious day I would be pleading guilty.

It was a ploy to stay out over Christmas and it worked. The trouble was, it sort of fucked Sellotape up - at the Magistrates court the most he could've got was six months. When we finally get to the Crown Court he's still pleading not guilty. I've changed my plea to guilty. Got meself a good probation report, and a spokesperson from the Alcohol Information Centre to speak for me. The best thing was, for me probation report I stole Sellotape's background as me own. I assumed the role of a product of a drunken marriage who was trying to come to terms with his own drinking. I even did two weeks in that role in a detoxification centre; better than two years in Strangeways. Anyway, when I get to the Crown, Justice Miller is pleased to see the steps I'm taking and I get a twelve month suspended sentence. Talk about a fucking scrum against the head.

Sellotape's up a fortnight later, and he's doing some village out of a fucking good idiot cos he's still pleading not guilty. For fuck's sake, they caught us in an opening with some of the gear and he's saying we were just there for a chat and didn't even notice the stuff there. As if. He's got no Probation reports cos he's too proud to crawl. No fucking defence case neither, the cunt defending him is Legal Aid and they ain't worth the money you don't pay them. You didn't need no Barnum of the Bailey to find him guilty.

I was in the Crown Court for the sentencing; thankfully my evidence wasn't needed - his solicitor thought it would damage his case (what fucking case? Heinrich Himmler had a better one). I was with Dodge, Bunny and this smarmy wanker called Durie.

Sellotape got three years - as they led him away he smiles at me. It wasn't a pleasant smile - more the sort that Fred West reserved for prospective lodgers.

122

Anyway, the spectators go for a drink in town. Bunny's crying and getting pissed, promising she'll wait for him forever cos he's the only man she's really loved. Durie's saying what a good lad Sellotape was, like the twat's dead. Dodge is saying nothing and I'm beginning to feel a right cunt. Forty-five minutes and two rounds later the poor fucker's forgot about. I'm coming back from the toilet and I see Bunny and Durie in the corridor by the side of the fruit machine. She's got his dick in her hand and her shirt's open and she's wearing her bra for a scarf. She's still got a fair pair of tits, I notice. I'm about ten feet away and they're talking like a fucking scene from *Love Story*. He's slurping at her tits and saying,

-I know this isn't the time or the place, but I've always had this thing about you, Denise.

She's handling his tosser like Steve Davis handles his snooker cue and saying,

-I love it when people call me Denise, nobody seems to remember my real name anymore.

Fucking great I'm thinking, her idea of foreplay is some wanker getting her fucking name right.

So as the song goes - I just walk on by- tell Dodge the score, drink up, and fuck off.

Dodge laughs and says,

-She's a rum fucker, so much for waiting forever.

Talk about, *Will You Still Love Me Tomorrow?*

That was it. That was the end of me lifelong friend, Sellotape. That is, until just over two years later when I go to Big Tony's flat. I knew something was wrong when I buzzed the Intercom. Three long blasts, two short blasts and one long blast. You've got to do it that way or Tony won't pick up the phone at his end.

-Who is it? he says.

-Rooftop, I say.

Then it goes a bit weird. There's nothing said for about thirty seconds, and he says,

-Push the door, Ronnie.

Now this cunt ain't called me Ronnie for more than fifteen years. So I push the door, walk in and start up the stairs to the tenth floor. I never get in them fucking lifts, they stink of piss and are always full of junkies' needles. Not only that, I'm always feared to fuck that the thing will get stuck and I'll have to spend a night in it. All the way up I'm thinking, what's the cunt found out?

When I finish me imitation of Sherpa Tensing I find his door open, so I walk right in and stroll into his living room. Its the same as always, littered with empty cans and what have you.

-Right big man, I say, fancy a pint or what?

He doesn't answer, just stands there combing his hair. I'm getting paranoid to fuck. The week before we bought and sold a combi boiler together. I told him I got two-fifty when I got three-fifty. I'm thinking he's found out the right price from Macca.

He turns to face me and says,

-John Reilly's out.

-Who? I say.

The cunt's took me by surprise. I'm thinking I've been caught at it and now he's changed the subject.

-A friend who wore Sellotape on his glasses twenty odd fucking year ago. Remember?

I start to get the fucking gist. Big Tony's visited Sellotape a couple of times in Haverigg. I ain't been meself. I mean, I ain't no fucking prison visitor. They have organisations for that. If he wants company he should find out what Lord fucking Longford's up to, or ring the Samaritans - them cunts were into chat lines before any fucker.

So I think Tony's having a bit of a pop at me for not going.

-Great, I say, let's call for him and I'll buy him a drink as well.

-Can't, he says.

I start to get the feeling that I'm playing Twenty fucking Questions. So I say,

-Let's cut a long story short - Miss Scarlet in the library with a candlestick?

Not a fucking murmur out of him. Then he goes over to his wall cabinet, picks a letter up and throws it to me.

So I read. It's headed, *My Life In A Stolen Moment, by John Reilly.*

I'm thinking I'm glad to see the cunt's still thieving, but Tony don't look like he's ready for what passes for wit with me, so I say fuck all. Anyway I've still got the sad bastard's letter, so here it is verbatim, as they say.

Dear Tony,

Thanks for visiting and that. As you can see by the postmark and the paper I'm out now. I'm not coming back to Manchester like I told you. I just want to keep on moving. I've just finished two years and I've been able to do a lot of thinking. Denise visited me twice; once out of curiosity and the second time to tell me she was having somebody else's love child. That's what she called it - a love child. It doesn't matter. I don't care and I certainly don't hate her. She had our Lee with her, and do you know what she said ? She said that they call him Sellotape in school. She thought that would cheer me up. It didn't; it made me think about us all. The poor kid, when Denise first had him nobody would believe that he was mine. The sad truth is that the poor kid is. When Denise had gone I thought about it all. All these people neatly labelled. Who are they? Sellotape, Permanently, Sozzled, Bunny, Superglue, Dodge, Egg and Bacon, and last but definitely least - Rooftop.

My name is John Reilly, not Sellotape. You know how I got called Sellotape? Not like everyone thinks. Yes, I did have Sellotape on my glasses all those years ago, but only for two days till they could get fixed. No, the real reason I became Sellotape was about a fortnight later I beat a boy called Ronnie Rafferty at a spelling test. When I went up to collect my prize dear old Rooftop shouted -Well done, Sellotape - and that was it - he made sure the name stuck better than Sellotape. If I would have lost to him I would have gone through the rest of my life being known as John Reilly. Every event from that test, to me getting three years and him getting a suspended sentence was an attempt to reverse that spelling test.

It took me a long time to realise that Mr Rafferty was an alien pretending to be a friend. He is a massive publicity machine, and the company he represents is himself. How did he become Rooftop? Sure, a Magistrate did call it him, and the Evening News did print it, but he must have bought fifty copies of that paper. He delivered more copies to more doors than the paperboy did. Then he started a graffiti campaign. Not your ordinary, 'United Rules OK' stuff. No, as part of his advertising campaign he put up weird slogans like 'La Tierra Esta La Notre. Rooftop.' on the side of the Post Office and 'All Profit Is Theft. Marx. All Theft Is Profit. Rooftop.' He got up at four in the morning to put that on the wall opposite the shops. Nice strategic positions, you notice. A month later everybody in the area knows who Rooftop is.

Why Rooftop? Well, it fitted in with his own pre-conceived opinion of himself. Don't get me wrong, the man's a genius. Take his fighting career. He won one totally ridiculous well publicised fight against a kid nobody could lose to, then he goes into retirement for the rest of his life. The kid he beats goes on to become a Priest - a touch of genius, picking that kid. If ten of us went to town and a fight broke out and Rooftop ran, it added to the myth. Remember when Robby Mooney got potted in the Portland Bars and Rafferty ran away. He actually turned that into a victory for his persona. He told Fat George that when he ran out all the lads thought he'd chased after the lad that done it, until they saw him overtake him on the stairs and keep going. Fat George told that story to everyone he served that day, and when Rafferty came back in the pub at the night, shares in Rooftop PLC were up ten percent.

All this sounds very bitter, and you might be thinking it's because I've just done two years and lost me wife, while Mr Rafferty has gone from strength to strength, but it isn't. I thank him for those two years. I've finally become me. I'm in Lindisfarne now, I don't know why. It's beautiful. I read a lot and write a bit. My brother James, the one they called Superglue, is practising medicine now in Glasgow. We talk on the phone often. Not a bad product of two drunks is he? Another myth that; although both my parents drank, neither drank as much as Rafferty's Dad. My Dad read Joyce, Keats, Shakespeare and Tolkien to us when we were kids, and I wish I could've thanked him for that before he died.

I won't write again Tony, but thanks for being you. Two favours I'll ask of you, Tony - one is never show this letter to anyone, and two - never call Mr Rafferty 'Rooftop' again.

Oh, before I close; the word he got wrong in the spelling test all those years ago was Sincerity. Bloody ironic that. Some American comedian once said that the most important thing in life was sincerity, and that once you'd learned how to fake that you were made. He should have met our charming friend.

Keep warm and remember Tony, if you ever get in between a man claiming to be a pacifist and something he wants, don't turn your back till you've hid the knives.

Your Friend

JOHN

P.S.— I hope you enjoy the mead.

I look up. Tony's staring at me like a Priest in a fucking confessional box. If he was waiting for me to say, 'Bless me Father for I have sinned,' he could fuck off. To be honest though I was well gutted. I mean, Sellotape had been to the same football game as me but we'd edited the highlights differently. The trouble was, Tony had been to the game as well and his version seemed to be leaning towards Sellotape's. Not only that, I thought we were all equally as close to each other; now I suddenly find that I'm outside the tent pissing in. Fuck the pair of them, I think.

There's a long pause,

-Well? says Tony.

I don't know what the cunt really expects me to say so I shrug and say,

-Any chance of any of that mead that he mentioned?

A smile crosses me face but there ain't no smile on Tony's. The gentle giant looks menacing, and I remember me Dad saying that if Tony ever put his mind to it he could be Heavyweight Champion of England with his build.

I fold the letter, put it in me pocket. Think to meself it's a fucking crying pity Sellotape didn't leave no forwarding address. Cos if he had, there would have been a dead rat winging its way to Lindisfarne C.O.D. same fucking day.

Tony's still combing his hair and waiting for some sort of response - I just say,

-See you.

And exit.

Give Tony his due though, the letter never got mentioned again. But the cagey fucker always called me Ronald after that.

SWOPSIES

So we start to do the Swopsies. It's a fucking arsehole of a job. Thank fuck it's Funny Red Nose Day. Robbie takes one of the bags and leaves the rest with me. So I'm stuck on a fucking bench with six bags of shopping, and a kid who's just learning how to walk and wants to show the world.

Rory looks at me and says,

-Dum Dum.

-Yeah I know, I say, I fucking must be to be stuck here.

I've got me eyes peeled for security guards but Robbie's back within minutes,

-No problems, give us another; burn the fuckers off then the first fucking train out, he says.

God, I fucking hate enthusiasm.

He bungs me the forty odd off the first hit and I'm thinking not that bad, at least I've got the price of a good dinner time piss up if anything goes wrong.

He fucks off for round two and I'm stuck on the fucking bench with Rory. The kid does seem out of sorts. Margery could be right, he could be coming down with a cold or something. Whatever the matter is I don't need him falling asleep on me when I do the Kiting. I need the little fucker on top of his game. I want him grabbing at the pen and making a general fucking nuisance of himself. That way no-one's really that bothered if me signature ain't a hundred percent. Cos it's fucking impossible to be holding a kid off with your left hand and writing with your right. I take out a bottle of orange and feed Rory a bit. It seems to perk him up a bit. If this don't work the little sod's going on black coffee.

I'm watching all the shoppers go by and I start getting lost in thought. I've lived all me life in Manchester and here I am sat in the middle of fucking Manchester

Arndale Centre, the hub of everything. Hundreds of people passing me on both sides, and I don't know any cunt. I'm thinking, what are the fucking odds against that? It makes you wonder though don't it. I mean, what percentage of people do I really know in me own City?

I'm well away on this useless train of thought when I see this Security Guard doing his rounds. I've nothing to fear, but he seems to me to be one of those cunts that care. He stops to chat to some woman shopper who appears to be asking directions. Keep him busy love, I'm thinking, as I start to pack stuff away. It's gone eleven now and there's no reason why I shouldn't be where I am with half a dozen shopping bags and a baby. I look just like any other married man waiting for his wife to finish her Friday morning shopping. But I'm paranoid to fuck, so I pick up me bags and try to get Rory to walk alongside me. The little twat's having none of it, and we're moving with all the speed and grace of a drunken Scotsman trying to get through an automatic door.

I've got Rory on me left arm and the bags in me right. I keep walking and don't look behind for Mr Three Pound an Hour. It's funny, but I've always had this survival instinct. Big Tony calls it absolute paranoia. I rely on it totally, and I've never been arrested sober.

Once at school this smart arse fucking science teacher took his watch off while he demonstrated some stupid thing. You know the kind of shite - red litmus paper turns blue, or some fucking thing. It made about as much sense to me as sticking a buttercup under some fucker's chin to see if they were in love.

Anyway, while all the would-be Barnes Wallis's were enthralled with his antics I walk over to the side of his table and pocket his watch. It's no great fucking piece or anything, it was just sort of on the spur of the moment. There's no real hassle if I see him looking round for it, I just say,

-Here it is, Sir,

and pass it off as a joke.

If he don't notice it's missing then it's home, James, and me Uncle Billy can either flog it or pawn it for me. I figure I'm in a no lose situation.

The lesson passes without the teacher Marsland noticing his time piece has gone, which chuffs me to fuck. I owe this cunt one, cos he once made the class form a circle holding hands, then passed an electric shock through us all. Not powerful enough to do us any harm, but powerful enough to shit the living daylights out of me.

The hooter goes and we go to the next class. I show Tony the watch on the way and we have a laugh about it. I should have followed the golden rule and stashed it but I couldn't be arsed. Everything's going fine; we're halfway through the next lesson when I spot the cunt of a science teacher Marsland at the door. He motions to the old twat who's teaching us, a cunt called Read, to come outside.

When Read leaves the room the usual shit happens - everyone's up and fucking about. Tony looks at me and I know that a man must do what a man must do. While all the arseholes are shouting back and forth to each other I walk as if to look out a window. As I pass a lad called Powell's desk, I slip the family silver into the cunt's coat pocket. I could just as easily have put the fucker behind the radiator or thrown it out of the window for that matter. But this way served two purposes - firstly the usual suspects, me and Tony, would be in the clear and secondly, I never did like the cunt Powell anyway. He was one of them too good to be true fuckers, always on the right side of the teacher. A clever fucker, but not now he wasn't. Now he was gonna learn a lesson a little bit more important than anything appertaining to fucking litmus paper.

Marsland and Read come back in, the noise

131

immediately stops and the fun and games start. Marsland is in his element. He gives a little speech saying a very important item has gone missing, and although he's accusing nobody we are all suspects. He wants to search us all - anybody not willing will be detained until the Police come. He asks if anybody has any objections. I toy with making this drama last until the end of school but think fuck it, if I do that I might miss Powell getting his just fucking rewards. We all agree to being searched. So Marsland says,

-Would everybody stand up please? Put your jackets on and stand with your hands by your sides.

We all comply.

-Now, he says, in two's starting front right, turn out the entire contents of your pockets.

He still hadn't explained to anyone what was missing so the class was bottling it in case they inadvertently had whatever it fucking was. I was shaking with anticipation. I couldn't wait till they cleared me and got the culprit. Me and Tony were about eight before Powell and the way it was being done was perfect for suspense.

Marsland does the two girls in front of us. They empty everything out of their pockets, fuck all worth having. I'm thinking of offering to frisk them, but there's no way I want to be sent out of the room.

-Thank you Susan and Caroline! he says - the way he says it you'd think they'd just finished a tap dance routine at the London Palladium.

Now it's mine and Tony's turn and I'm thinking he's only gone through a pantomime with the rest of the class - if the cunt could lay odds, me and Tony would lead the field. Well, this time he's gonna be disappointed. He looks at us and says,

-Rafferty and Nicholls - pockets.

I empty a pound in change and Tony empties a couple of coins and a comb. There's a look of

132

disappointment on Marsland's face.

Tony looks at all me change on the table and says,

-You sod - I bought you chips at dinner cos you said you were skint.

This cracks the class up. Till Marsland screams,

-QUIET!

The poor cunt's losing it. He's well had the piss taken out of him. Then as a last resort he says,

-You'll all be here until it's sorted.

Big fucking deal - this is Tuesday, and this has got to be more interesting than me Mam's pea soup.

There's a girl, Janet Brearley, crying at the front of the class. Soft cow - if I'd have had the chance I'd have slipped the fucking thing in her pocket; that would have given her something to cry for.

Then it's Powell's turn. I couldn't resist turning to look what's going on. He dips his hand in his pocket, and the look on his face is one of absolute horror. He pulls out the watch and he's holding it there in mid air. He's guessed he's found the Holy Grail and he's locked between puzzlement and fear. I'm thinking safest thing to do wanker, is panic. Marsland's staring at him, his eyeballs coming out of his head. Every eye in the class is on Powell. Three years of impeccable behaviour down the drain for one moment of madness. I wouldn't mind, but it wasn't even his fucking moment.

He looks at Marsland and starts crying. Too late for that shite now, take it like a fucking man. He starts stammering,

-No Sir, it wasn't me Sir, no Sir.

I start feeling sorry for the cowardly cunt. Truth is I hate to see any fucker caught.

Marsland grabs him and tries to haul him out of the class. But Powell's got a grip on the desk and he's fighting every inch of the way. He's sobbing now, and its barely audible what he's saying,

-No Sir, I didn't, honest Sir.

He starts screaming. It's getting fucking embarrassing. Then he allows himself to be led away. He's got his head sort of bowed down with all the shame.

The old twat Read goes out with Marsland and Powell and they leave a cocky shit called Glover in charge of the class. Glover is Powell's best mate.

As soon as the pair of wank teachers go all hell breaks loose.

-Hey Glover, shouts Tony, you better hope that Powell keeps his trap shut, cos if he says that the two of you were in it together you're up Shit Street too!

You should see the look on Glover's face - the cunt is genuinely worried that his mate might nominate him for a supporting actor role. I tell the class that Powell's Mam has gone off with the man from next door, and that he's probably only took to thieving so he can get some attention.

Janet Brearley's still crying so Tony goes to comfort her. Which leads to a predictable scream as he tries to grope her.

It might sound ridiculous but it did Powell the world of good. He became a known character after that, and regarded as a bit of a slippery customer. He even started knocking round with me and Tony for a while. The thing I couldn't handle was the way the cunt kept boasting about how he'd took the fucking watch!

Anyway, this cunt of a Security guard was heading my way. So I'm walking lob sided trying to carry Rory and the bags. In a situation like this there's only one answer - I head for the safety of the John Willie's pub and a pint of bitter.

There's no fucker in - just the way I like it. So I'm sat there relaxing, half way down a pint trying to plot me next move. I've seen enough of this day already; I don't need no more shite, I decide. Fuck Robbie, I'll get a taxi home, drop off Rory me baby faced accomplice, and the bags. Take the forty, tell Margery that me and

Robbie have been separated. Say I'm off to make sure he ain't been nicked. Then fuck off in the Church. Have twenty on a horse, a few pints, and go back home with a bottle of vodka. I'm just about to neck the remainder of me bitter when I look up and clock a big gap tooth smile at the door.

It's Robbie - he walks over, smiling like fuck.

-You've found me, I say, - now it's your fucking turn to hide.

He sits himself down next to me and says,

-Get us a pint of fucking orange.

I tell him to fuck off and take another bag with him.

DRINKIN

The biggest bollock I dropped in me whole life was the shite at the Pack Horse, and how I got away with it I'll never fucking know. It's the only time I've ever allowed meself to get involved with anything that even loosely involves violence. In fact, the legal term for the fucking mess is Aggravated Robbery. To be honest though, all the violence consisted of on my part was empty threats. I didn't have a fucking intention of doing fuck all. Mind you, I can't speak for the others.

It all started innocently enough. I'd been out with me Uncle Billy Kelly in the afternoon. Billy's game was hanging round bus stations and train stations or any fucking place where people gathered with luggage. He was like some sort of frustrated fucking bellboy. He lived in a Tower Block in Monsall and his motto was,

-Breakfast in Manchester, lunch in Munich, luggage in Monsall.

He was good at what he did, and he made a sorted living at it. Apart from the obvious fact that he was a known man to the Dirty and a suitcase couldn't go missing this side of Carlisle without some 'Gates of The Yard' wanted to interview Billy about it. I'd bumped into him on Swan Street about four o'clock in the afternoon. I had fuck all money and fuck all to do, so I went with him for the crack.

So we're standing outside the Midland Hotel and Billy's surveying everything that moves. I'm bored to fuck, thinking I wonder if the cunt's got any money and more to the point, if he has, will he lend it me? Then Billy taps me on the shoulder, points to this suited wanker getting out of a taxi and says,

-Wait here and don't move. When I come out give it thirty seconds and make sure I ain't being followed.

I think to meself that the cunt is being a bit melodramatic but I've got fuck all else to do, and anyway he can be as tricky as a Harlem Globetrotter, so I nod and lean against the wall.

The suited tosser pays his taxi and don't take no change, so he looks like he's a good tipper. He's a typical Mr Cut and Blow Dry - some sort of fucking salesman on a freebie from his company. He walks into the hotel not even noticing that he's being man for man marked by the best since Nobby Stiles.

I'm outside maybe five or ten minutes before Billy comes out with the man's case. He's moving like a West Indian fast bowler on a good wicket. But I do as I'm instructed and I give it enough time to make sure he ain't been noticed, which he hasn't. He's sold Mr Salesman a dummy. I trot after him fast enough to catch him but not fast enough to attract the curse of the thieving classes, the have-a-go fucking hero. He can shift a bit for a man in his fifties, but I join up with him the other side of Piccadilly Gardens.

-No problems, I say, no one came after you.

We jump a bus on Oldham Street and he's hugging the fucking case like it's the FA Cup. I've never seen the cunt so excited and I realise he ain't in it for the money, it's the fucking excitement. Oh well, it takes all fucking sorts.

We get back to the Heywood. Billy walks over to a table, places the case down and says,

-I rest my case!

I've heard that gem about a million times before, so I tap him for the price of two pints and get the beer in while he's fucking with the locks. I get back with the beer and we move into the Vault, which is empty. The case has a sort of three number combination lock on each side of the handles.

I start badgering Billy to get the cunt open, and he cracks another one of his standard jokes.

-Don't worry son, he says, this will soon be an open and shut case.

Me patience is wearing thin. I'm thinking about the wages that could be inside the fucker. So I say,

-Break the fucking locks.

A look of total disgust crosses his face.

-Break the fucking locks! he mimics; this is a pure leather case. If there's fuck all worth having inside it at least we'll get twenty for it. What we do is crack the combination.

I fall about laughing. The mad old cunt has been watching too much James Bond. He's finally snapped - now he thinks he's a fucking safe cracker. Fuck it I think, I might as well humour him - after all it was him that had the fucker away.

So I'm sat there drinking me bitter and cursing the loony. I'm thinking any minute now he's gonna give in and let the forgotten art of wanton vandalism reign supreme. Then out of the blue the fucking thing goes 'Click', and one side of the combination flirts open.

-OK Jason King, I say, how the fuck did you do that?

He ignores the insult and carries on with his case. I'm thinking the fucker will be easy to open now, all I've got to do is borrow a screwdriver off the landlord and prise it.

-Come on Billy, you're never gonna guess it, I say.

But he's working like a man on piece time. The little dials are spinning forty to the fucking dozen. Just when I think him getting the first part was a bigger fluke than an England Ashes win, the second one goes 'Click'.

Billy sits back - the cat that got the fucking cream.

-Fair play to you, I say, how'd you do it?

He says nothing. The case is sat there, both metal fasteners in the air like a whore's legs. He ain't making no attempt to open the lid and I know why - he's about to fucking start preaching. He sips his beer, then he starts:

-If you'd ever bothered to go to school instead of hanging round the streets shoplifting, you'd know that there are only nine hundred and ninety nine possible combinations of three numbers. So put the fucker on 999, hope no cunt's ringing it, and work your way backwards and hey presto! a rabbit everytime, he says.

-Nice one, I say - open the fucker.

Billy opens it and all there is are assorted clothes, a couple of books, a bunch of letters, a shaver and a calculator. I pick the letters up and start to read one and Billy throws a fucking wobbler,

-Put that down - a man's business is his own!

I think to meself, it fucking would be if some thieving toe rag didn't do a runner with it.

Give Billy his due, he knew his game; the case was floggable and we got fifteen quid for it from the board man in the bookies opposite. Billy gave me seven and a half plus the shaver, which was very fair cos he'd done all the work.

We have a couple of pints together then he fucks off home to me Aunt Betty. God, that woman had a tortured life with him. One time they're on Victoria Station waiting for the Blackpool train. They were off for a fortnight's holiday and Billy's got hold of two suitcases, both his own, when the Railway Police swoop and arrest him and me Aunt Betty. They know Billy well, and when their video camera picks him up carrying cases they immediately think he's in possession of a couple of earners. Four fucking hours in custody and they finally release him with an apology.

Anyway I'm left with about four quid. So I think fuck it, I'll have another and see if I can catch Badger and Freddie in the Pack Horse. I try to tap Fat George but he's having none of it so I bung him the shaver as a present and fuck off down the Pack.

I get there at about seven o'clock and Badger and Freddie are already in. I shout to Badger as I walk through the door; he's at the bar so he gets me a pint in. When he sits down I explain I can't get a round back cos I'm out of the game. Badger says no matter cos he's in the landlord's ribs. By this I think he means he's tapped him for ten or twenty, but he explains that Gilly the landlord is letting him run up a slate. I think to meself, this is absolute fucking madness. Gilly has got to be out of his shed. There's three of us now in a round and he's given a lush like Badger an open cheque at the bar.

-Where the fuck is he? I say.

-Fuck knows, says Freddie; he put on a suit and fucked off out.

It's obvious to anyone that knows the three of us that we're gonna drink till we're either too fucked to manage anymore, or some cunt stops us. It's also equally obvious that we ain't gonna pay the bill. But if Gilly wants to make a cunt of himself, so be it.

He wasn't one of us anyway. He'd come down from Cumbria and made himself out to be some sort of hard man. Then he'd just stood there when two Cheetham lads came into his pub and took his machines. He actually watched them load the fuckers into a van and never even rang the Dirties till there was a puff of smoke as they drove away. That was a big mistake - he'd just used his body language to tell every fucker within a five mile radius that he was a soft fucking touch. His only hope henceforth in the on-going situation of life as it is in Miles Platting was to do a Viraj Mendis in the Church next door. Cos there was a Fatwah on him, and it was odds on he was gonna get turned over. That's probably why he gave Badger the open cheque. He must have figured that with Badger being six foot odd he was buying some protection. Whatever the reason, it proved suicidal.

We'd all started drinking bottles of Pils. It's funny how many and how fast you can drink when it's free and the landlord's due back any minute and could put a stop to it.

We have a couple more. I'm feeling generous so I give the lads me four quid for the cigarette machine and the jukebox. It's blaring out, *Like A Rolling Stone*, when Robbie walks in.

He's been on the Mooch to Huddersfield and he's made a couple of bob, but Badger tells him to put it away, it's his treat. By this time it's in for a penny, in for a pound.

God fucking knows now what the tick bill is, but then again who cares, cos we ain't gonna pay. I'm anticipating getting barred, but big fucking deal there's plenty more pubs on Oldham Road, and if I'm barred me mates are coming with me. It's pig at a trough time. I go to the bar, order the same again plus four gin and oranges. The barmaid, Young Julie, is a quivering wreck; she don't want to serve me but I say,

-It's sorted - Badger's OK'd it.

She looks over at the big man as if he's the landlord. Badger waves and she serves me. I take it all back on a tray, and I'm thinking the way things are going we'll need a dustbin lid for the next round.

At the table there's only Robbie who's anywhere near sober. As I get back Freddie's saying,

-He's been fair to us, has Gilly. We can't let him down; we'll get a tick list off Julie. Split it four ways and pay him back next time we have an earner. Can't make a cunt out of a man who's been as fair as him.

We're all nodding but I'm thinking, like fuck we will. I've got no intention of paying Gilly anything and I know for a fact that none of the other fuckers have.

Badger, mein host at the Last Supper, is saying,

-I can say with impunity that this bill will be paid.

Now I know the cunt is drunk - when he's past his sell by date every sentence includes -'with impunity'.

Robbie tells us about his day. He got caught in a cabin on a site by two Irish lads. They got him bang to rights going through a jacket. No fucking ringing the

Dirties, just a couple of whacks. Like Robbie said, better that way, saves on the paper work.

-I copped lovely in a mill afterwards, he says; I walked past the reception and I'm heading down this corridor. There's glass doors on both sides. Full of typists and other arseholes fucking about. I see this one office empty so I duck in. I go through this tart's jacket. I get thirty quid out of her coat. I'm just pocketing the fucker when she comes back. She ain't seen nothing so I start asking if there's any work. She's a snooty bitch and she fucks me off. I'm thinking to meself, fuck you - I've got your rent money in me pocket. The cow asks a fucking Guard to escort me off the premises. I walk out, don't give a fuck. The Security Guard says fuck her, she's a dyke, and I'm on the train and fucking off home.

As Robbie's talking, Gilly comes back, spots us at our table and comes right over. He's been to some licensee thing, Victuallers, some such shite. He's half pissed and he wants to get the beer in, but Freddie says,

-No, I'll get these.

And before Gilly can argue he picks up the tray and heads for the bar. A wise move I'm thinking, cos as soon as Julie behind the bar shows Gilly the Third World Debt that's our bar bill, he's gonna put the towels on.

Anyway we keep the cunt at our table till near last orders. He thinks we're getting the beer in, which we are; but what he don't realise, as Jeremy fucking Beadle would say, is that he's being had, cos in the long run he's paying himself.

After about an hour and three or four drinks, Gilly has had enough of our company and decides he's got to help poor Julie who's run off her feet. When he gets to the bar Julie shows him a piece of paper with our debt on it. I say piece of paper - it's more like a fucking toilet roll. They both look over - Badger smiles and shouts across,

-Monday morning - I'm expecting a cheque.

We're down near the bottom of our glasses and we're all pissed. Badger says,

-Let's have another for the road.

We all agree but none of us have the bottle for the hassle at the bar. In the end Freddie goes up. We can see he's having a bit of trouble with Gilly, but Freddie's a silver tongued fucker and he finally returns to base with four bottles of Pils and four vodkas.

-What's he say? asks Robbie.

-Says it's what the cobbler threw at his wife.

I don't need to ask Freddie to explain the riddle, the answer's simple enough - it's the last.

-Like fuck, I say.

I'm a stubborn little fucker when I'm pissed.

The pub's now empty and we're downing the dregs of our last drink. Freddie says,

-Let's ask him for a carryout.

We all nod and wait.

Gilly comes over collecting glasses.

-Come on lads, he says, I've got to lock up - get a move on.

-Give us a carry out, says Badger.

That's when it got out of hand. Gilly refuses us flatly. But it's too late. If he'd have said no in front of a half full pub, our hands would've been tied, we couldn't have done fuck all. Now it's getting on for midnight and there's only us, him and Young Julie. Julie immediately reads the situation and fucks off home to her boyfriend and baby. If you ain't seen nothing then you don't know nothing.

Gilly's reeling under the pressure. The cunt ain't got the bottle for it. I'll tell you what, I could carve a better man out of a fucking banana.

-You can have twelve cans of lager and that's it, he says.

If we'd have been sober we'd have thanked the man

but we ain't sober, we're drunk, so we're gonna fuck the man.

-Throw a bottle of vodka in as well, I say.

Gilly looks at me and you can tell he don't rate me. He knows I don't fight, but he's missed the essential difference between me and him; you have to kick me to death before you take anything that's mine. He decides to make his stand with me.

-Don't be a cunt all your life, he says.

And that's it - we're past the point of no return, as me old driving instructor used to say. So it's foot down and fuck everyone else. I point to the big optic vodka bottle and say,

-I want that.

-Fuck you, says Gilly, no way.

But it's too late baby now - Freddie just walks round and takes it down, puts it on the bar, then he does the same with the optic gin.

Robbie, who's been watching all and saying fuck all, shouts,

-Fuck that, pass me the till!

The till drawer has already been taken out and put near the cigs. Freddie does what Robbie says and puts it on the bar. Gilly makes a frantic grab for the fucker. Robbie gets it the same time, looks Gilly straight in the eye and says,

-Don't.

Gilly has the fucking sense to let go before Robbie makes him.

Me bottle's gone - all I wanted was a drink after time. This load of shit is well out of order; if we get nailed for this it's serious time, and no fucking about.

Badger gets the vodka and the gin. Robbie's got the till. Freddie's getting as many cigs as he can carry and I'm stood there watching it all go on. Freddie takes command. I'm glad to see that some fucker's still got his brain in operation.

-Rooftop, stay with Gilly, I'll be back in a minute. You two, with me.

The three of them exit stage right and I'm left with Gilly. I'm shitting meself - he's twice me size and now I'm on me own with him. What the fuck's going on? I'm wondering whether to do one or not. Then the cunt starts crying. I'll tell you, he beat me to it by about thirty fucking seconds. I'm stood in between him and the door and I'm holding him. God knows why, cos if he wants to make a run for it, I ain't gonna fucking stop him. In fact, I'd be right behind him. Me head's starting to come back together.

He's moaning,

-It's me livelihood. I'll lose me job and me house.

I try to reason with him, it's our only fucking chance.

-Listen, I say, nobody but you knows what was in that till. Screw the fucking insurance and the brewery. Whatever you're owed in tick bills, say that was in the till. Put a bit more on for yourself. Who gives a fuck?

He's listening; thank fuck the bottleless bastard has got a brain. So I carry on,

-If they get any of us and it's through you, then you're dead meat. We all work for Davis, and you know Davis will get you if it takes ten fucking years. Plus a couple of them others are dangerous bastards in their own right. Fuck with us and it ain't just you - it's your wife and kids that have to worry.

I'm talking a load of bollocks but he don't know that.

Freddie comes back and he shouts me. Before I go, I say,

-Remember. Screw the insurance. Why get hurt ?

Me and Freddie leg it on to the estate. I think he's got a car waiting but he fucking ain't. He takes me to the rest of the Lavender Hill Mob - they're waiting in a maisonette opening. The nearest house is Robbie's. So we dump the till drawer down the rubbish chute and head for there. We split up into twos.

I'm with Badger. Robbie takes all the notes, Freddie has the cigs, I pocket all the shrapnel and Badger grabs the spirits. We aim for Robbie's house in different directions. It's obvious Gilly ain't rang the Dirties yet cos we cross Miles Platting and they ain't about. Badger is walking along swigging raw vodka and I'm doing the same with the gin. Fuck knows how we made it to Robbie's.

When we get there we have a bit of a sort out. It's odds on that Freddie and Robbie have had a dip into the notes, but that's fair play - nothing me and Badger wouldn't have done in the same circumstances. What the fuck, me and him have carved up most of the pound coins between us, and seeing as we're greedier twats than them it's probably swings and roundabouts.

It's a good hoist; it works out at about four hundred and sixty pound each.

-It would've been fucking double if we'd paid for our beer, says Robbie.

It's party time; we sit back and start on the vodka and gin. Everything's going great, then the women arrive. At first it's just Clarissa and Freddie's girlfriend Sharon, which ain't that bad. Then they find out what we've done and are trying to make us see the shit we're in. Sharon starts shouting at Freddie,

-You stupid fucking bastards! Everyone in there tonight will know tomorrow who it was that fucking done it! You bunch of fucking clowns, the Dirty will be round here first thing in the fucking morning!

Clarissa is giving Robbie the same sort of shite.

I'm swigging away the memory on gin and orange. It all gets a little bit blurred. Somewhere in there Margery arrives in a taxi. I'm too drunk to give a fuck. I close my eyes and I feel this terrible pain, like someone's got a grip of my hair. I don't want to open the fuckers cos I know when I do, I will be staring at Margery.

I finally do open me eyes and I am staring at Margery

- but it's the next morning, and fuck knows how I got home. I lie there thinking about what happened in the Pack, and I think fuck me - I'm gonna end up doing two fucking years for four hundred and sixty fucking quid. I figure it out; it works out to two hundred and thirty a year, nine fucking teen a month, and four pound-odd a week. Not even a pound a fucking day. I'm depressing meself with this line of thought when a car pulls up outside. I think fuck it - if it's on top, it's on top. I ain't gonna run over no rooftops shouting, 'you'll never take me alive, Copper.' I look out the window; it's Robbie and Clarissa getting out of a taxi. I leave Margery in bed, sling an old football shirt and jeans on and fuck off down stairs to answer it.

They've been up all night. Robbie hadn't drank as much as the rest of us and Clarissa had made him see what stupid cunts we'd all been. I'm sober now and no one has to tell me what a fucking major bollock has been dropped. It's too late now to do fuck all about it. What's done is done, but all I fucking wanted was a carryout. Now we're all up to our eyeballs in Aggravated fucking Robbery.

-We're in deep shit, I say.

-It ain't that bad, says Robbie.

I look at him and wonder what his idea of bad is.

-We assaulted him, I say.

-Bollocks, says Robbie, nobody touched him.

-I fucking held him, I say, which as any lawyer will tell you means we all held him, and that is fucking assault. We all get time for it if it comes on top.

Margery comes downstairs,

-What's up? she says.

-The seasonally adjusted figures on unemployment, what the fuck do you think? I say.

-You won't be so fucking cocky when the Dirty arrive, she says, and the smile leaves me face as fast as an Italian forward from a relegated team.

-OK, I say, gimme a fucking break will you ?

-A fucking break? You want your fucking legs breaking that's what you want, you stupid cunt.

And this I don't fucking need. I slump down on the recently bumped couch with me head in me hands.

-I was doing it for you and the kids, I lie.

-Cheers, she sneers, the babies can have the vodka and I'll have the gin.

I don't answer cos there ain't no answer apart from the power of prayer and me hotline to God got disconnected round about the time I had it away with a St Joseph's penny box from Corpus Christi church.

-And another thing, Margery adds, get all the stuff out of the shed- cos if the Dirty see that they'll open the fucker up as an incident room.

-Calm down, I say getting annoyed, act fucking normal.

At this she loses it completely.

-Act fucking normal! How the fuck would you know what normal is? You set the fucking alarm clock for four a fucking clock last week so you could get up and drink cunting vodka before you went to work. You ain't fucking normal. Nothing in this fucking house is normal.

I ask her if there's anything to drink and she gives me the baby's cup with a sigh. It's a little blue plastic thing with a lid on. Inside is the last of the Pack Horse gin. I've got some lemonade in the fridge, so me life's sorted for the next thirty fucking minutes. I'm swigging like a condemned man - there's fuck all left to do but wait.

Gilly knows all our names, or enough about us to have had the Dirty here by now. Maybe he's being sensible and keeping his mouth shut, but even if he is, Young Julie might not. Not only that, but a minimum of a hundred people saw us in the Pack last night. If the Dirty ask enough questions, we're fucked.

It's a twat of a situation. We know it was a drunken piss up that got out of hand but you convince a fucking Judge that four men against one after last orders was anything but premeditated robbery. We also warned him of the consequences of going to the Dirty, and in anybody's book that smacks of gangsterism. No - if this comes to court we'll all get three fucking years. Margery and Clarissa are calling us every cunt's name you can think of, and I had to fucking agree.

Me and Robbie gave Miles Platting a wide berth at dinner time and went in the Church in Newton Heath for a few pints and a game of pool. It was a pretty miserable dinner time - I was expecting the phone to go at any time, and Margery to tell me that the Dirty had been.

We get back to my house at about four o'clock, well pissed, and there's still no sign of the Dirty. Freddie's been on the phone - the Pack has been dubbed up all day and he's been round to see Julie. According to her, she's seen Gilly and he's spent three hours in Collyhurst nick. He's been shown all the mug shots and he can't recognise no fucker. It's good news so far - if Gilly has done that we're more than half way in the clear. He can't suddenly go back on his testimony and recognise four people he knows well unless he claims intimidation. Also if Julie's telling Freddie all this, then she ain't gonna tell the Dirties fuck all. It's beginning to look like Gilly has used his head and decided to make the insurance company pay for his mistake. Fair play to the man, it's nothing that Mr Fucking Average don't do every day of the week. Nobody's seen Badger - it looks like he's took his money and done one. He won't show up again till he's boozed his four and a half.

The next few days were fucking torture. Every fucking knock on the door, every fucking car pulling up was agony. I was living on pins. But I knew that every day that went by made us a little bit safer.

The Pack opened up in the middle of the next week under relief management. They hadn't sacked Gilly, they'd just moved him on. Badger resurfaced about a week later, and that was the end of it. We never heard fuck all more. Looking back though, that was the one occasion when I know God was on my side. He must've thought to himself - Naw, the lads don't mean it.

I seen Gilly once after that. It was about two years later. I walked into a pub somewhere near Swinton, and the cowardly cunt was running it. He looked across at me and we immediately recognised each other. Fuck all was said. I sat down with the lads I was with and said,

-Drink this. I know a better place round the corner.

A FIREPLACE REMEMBERED

We were walking through this sort of garden area at the back of the C.I.S. and he wouldn't stop fucking gabbing. He was going on and on about City, and how they were on the brink of something big, with all the good young kids they were signing. I'm thinking like fuck they are, the only thing worth pinching in their fucking trophy room is the fucking carpet. I'll tell you, me head was all over the place with him.

Then it happened. I spotted what I first took to be two male tramps, but as we got nearer I realised it was a man and a woman. They were sort of half sitting, half lying on a bench. As we approached, one of the bundle of rags went into his routine. He was Scots, and judging by his style he'd done an Open University degree in Aggressive Begging.

-Hey you, have you gorra ciggy? he says in a Glasgow accent.

Not so much a question, more a statement of intent. Robbie smiled and passed him one. As he did so the other bundle of rags, a female rose (as in got up, not the fucking flower). The Scotsman was thanking Robbie profusely for his act of generosity,

-Cheers Ace, he says, we've no had a chance tae go to the shop yet!

He said it like he'd just got out of bed and he was about to Hoover the living room carpet when a couple of neighbours had dropped in.

Robbie gave the second part of the rag-tag team a cig. I'll give him his due; if some fucker was worse off than him, he'd not see them short. Fucking weakness I call it. Anyway, he gives the girl the cigarette. She lights it and turns to me. We both recognise each other immediately. She sort of nods and says,

-Lo Ron, long time no see.

She still had a middle class Cheadle accent.

-Hi, I say.

Though I remember her, for the fucking life of me I couldn't think of her name. I'd met Wotshername about eight years previously. Me and a lad I knocked about with, Maurice, used to hang around the Electric Circus in Collyhurst. We were mainly after a fuck, but mainly getting fucked off.

Anyway, we cop for Wotshername one night at the Circus when she's too stoned to care. We take her back to this Tower Block in Blackley where she lives. Talk about fucking dreary! She had fucking nothing; just an old cooker, a wanked out mattress and two bags of clothes. So, she puts on some water to make tea and all she had to boil it in was an old bean tin,

-Advertising for Heinz? Maurice says.

No fucking smile from her, no nothing. At this stage I'm thinking she's making some sort of statement against wealth. That she's one of them middle class types playing silly fucking games, like the Socialist Workers do before they become Doctors and Dentists. I open the cupboard - there's about half a dozen tea bags, a drop of milk and a tin of cat food. No sign of no cat, so that don't bear thinking about. I laugh and say,

-If the Red Cross find out they'll start flying food in.

Again no response. Oh well I think, me working class humour's a bit beneath her.

She finishes brewing up and we sit down talking. At this point it's even money whether Wilson or Keppel finishes up with Betty. Then fuck me, it's tears before fucking bedtime. She tells us her life story. Her Dad, and I use that term fucking loosely, is doing eight years for fucking her. He'd been doing it to her since as early as she can remember. He's in Walton and she still writes to him. He's also been doing the same to her two sisters.

While she's telling us all this she's looking into space, and Maurice has got her down on the mattress. He's got her tits out and he's undoing her jeans. She seems as unperturbed by Maurice's sexual advances as she does by the story.

I listen to this shit for about half an hour and I decide to get me head down. There's only so many times a man can tut in horror without getting pissed off. Maurice and Wotshername have commandeered the mattress, so I pinch his Columbo mac for a quilt, and I get me head down in the bath. The next morning he comes into the bathroom. He didn't need to wake me up - she was such a weird fucker that I'd slept with one eye open just in case she put a pair of scissors through me chest. Daft really; where would she get a pair of scissors from?

-How was it? I say.

OK, says Maurice. Then he smiles and adds,

-She could've been reading the Football Pink while I did it, for all the interest she took.

-Screwed her then? I say, trying to illicit some more details.

-I did nothing her own Father wouldn't have done, the cruel bastard says.

I laugh and he says,

-Why don't you go in now and flirt her one?

I'm well fucking offended. I say,

-No, I rather open the batting or stay in the pavilion.

I get up and we go back into the living room. Wotshername is in a state of undress. She's taking one dirty outfit off and putting another dirty one on.

-Got any money for cigs and milk? she says.

I shrug. Fuck off, I think. Maurice did the screwing, let him do the paying.

-Yeah, says Maurice - come on, we'll nip to the shops.

So Bonny and Clyde leave me there to make a bean tin brew and go through her worldly goods. Not a lot of going through really. I'm sorted at sneak thieving - I can go through a room, open, examine and return everything and you wouldn't know a thing had been touched.

Anyway, there's fuck all of interest. A couple of personal things, a medical card and a letter from some 'Uncle'. The letter is a classic; he says how much he loves her, promises her all sorts, and finishes up apologising for what happened at Belle Vue Dogs. I'm reading between the lines but I'm fairly fucking certain he wasn't apologising for putting their bus fare on the last favourite.

So I'm sat down waiting for the return of the Lovers when the door goes. I've fuck all else to do, so I go to answer it. It's the mail - a postcard from North Manchester General Hospital inviting her for a check up (Christ, I'm thinking - I hope she's got a dose of the clap. That'll fuck that smart arse Maurice up) and a letter from the Social. Being a firm believer in the freedom of information (especially other people's) I open the fucker. Somewhere far off a jukebox is playing my song. In it is a Giro for forty eight quid and a letter explaining what it's for. So I pocket both, nip back to her bag and borrow the Medical Card - that'll do for ID at the post office.

Now I'm bouncing like an Harlem Globetrotter's ball - all I have to do is wait for the shoppers to return, hang round for half an hour, tap Maurice for me bus fare, the less that twat knows the better, and I'm off down the Rochdale Road. It might seem like a shit trick taking her money but not really - the stuck up cow's got a Mother at home in Cheadle who'll give her anything she wants, apart from love. She's also got Social Workers and support groups on her case, and them cunts can get you a grant for a lawn mower if you live on the tenth fucking floor. What did I have ? A fucking Probation Officer who kept threatening to breach me if I missed another session. Everyone she'd met in life so far had fucked Wotshername. I'd just done it a little different - I hadn't used me knob.

Mills and Boon come back and he's all fucking over her. It must be love cos he's got some shopping in. It's obvious he's planning to stay a day or so by what he's bought, which suits me cos he'll be in the frame for the Giro.

I give them a brew each. Maurice gets out a packet of Jaffa Cakes. I remember the hospital card, and think - I hope they're penicillin flavoured. Maurice says,

-It would be all right this place, if it had a stick or two of furniture.

That does it for me. I'm fucked if I'm gonna listen to Mr fucking Blandings build his dream house. So I tap Maurice for me bus fare, and in the words of many a *News of the World* journalist, I made my excuses and left.

I got Mary to cash the giro using the Medical Card as ID. I told her it was for some girl out of the Osborne, bunged her the spare eight quid and fucked off on the piss.

Anyway, here I am years later staring her in the face. She ain't changed a lot, which ain't really much of a compliment to pay a tramp you've not seen since pre-tramp days.

 I say,

-How you doing?

I feel a cunt the second I've said it. I mean, what a stupid fucking question.

-OK, she says - got any money?

I don't know if it's guilt about the Giro or just fear that one day I might be in her shoes (size threes, tongue out, sole adrift) but I delve in me pocket, pull out a fiver and give it to her.

-Thanks Ron, she says, turns to the Scotsman, who's deliriously happy, and gives him the fiver. He looks at me, clears his throat, and I think the cunt's about to make an acceptance speech. But he's brief.

-Cheers Ace, he says, and they turn away.

155

Me and Robbie walk on a bit.

-God Rooftop, you've knocked about with some iffy fucking women, he says. -Who the fuck was that?

I laugh and say, -Oh, just some girl who's Giro I had away a few year ago.

-Before or after you fucked her? he says.

-Neither, I say - instead of.

We walk off towards the station.

-You bastard, Robbie says.

But he's laughing and so am I.

We're walking past this suited wanker carrying a mobile phone. Posing cunt you can tell his name is Nigel or Giles just by the way he talks. Robbie takes one look at the twat and says,

-Close that deal but get it in Yen!

Nigel or Giles ain't got a clue what's going on, he moves his phone away from his ear.

-Get out of derivatives and into women's underwear, I say.

-Sorry, the Young Investor of the Year says as he pushes past us, but he fucking ain't.

Fucking cunt, I think, he'd have died in revolutionary Russia - one look at his segless fucking hands and it would've been,

-Do you want a blindfold, Comrade?

I'm thinking to meself that it's a small world bumping into Wotshername again. Then again it ain't really, cos the first girl I ever screwed walks past me often. She's like most people from round our area - they never seem to move away. All live within two miles of where they were born. All except Sellotape and Superglue, and they're a pair of fucking headbangers so they don't fucking count. It's as if we're all still kids playing hide and seek, and we daren't go beyond the boundaries of certain roads in case our Mams call us in for our dinner.

Maureen Bailey her name was - still is. The first girl I ever had carnal knowledge of. Everybody called her

Little Mo, after some fucking tennis player. Though her game was a bit different it still featured a bit of the old 'New balls please'. It's a little hard to describe her, as she was one of them nondescript sort of girls. She never went to school but she always wore a school uniform. Yellow blouse with a brown skirt - she looked like an over ripe banana. Her hair was sort of brown, with the front dyed blonde which was her idea of a fashion statement. Spindly legs and no tits, but she was hugely popular with the boys cos she did a turn.

Anyway this day I'm walking past her house and she comes to the door. I've known her for years, she's in the class below me at St Martin's, but we've never really talked. It's like that when you're at school - if someone is a year below you it's like you're Indians and they're in a different caste - you wouldn't be seen dead talking to them.

She looks at me, smiles, and says,

-Wagging it?

-Yeah, I say.

Normally I'd tell her to fuck off, but I'm on me own cos Vinny and Sellotape's in Rosehill. I can't find Big Tony anywhere, so I've fuck all else to do but talk to her.

-Wanna come in? she says.

I give a look as if to say I'm not fucking arsed, but I follow her in. It'll kill a bit of time till four o'clock. It's a really nice house, better than ours. Her Dad makes home brew beer, so she asks if I want a cupful. I say,

-Yeah.

She gives me a big mug full of the stuff. I have a swig and it tastes vile, all hops, but I want to look like a big man so I just wallop it back and say,

-Fucking great!

She points to the swear box, and says that if her Dad was here I'd have to put money in the fucker. We both fall about laughing, saying fuck this and cunt that.

We sit on the floor playing Ludo. We have two teams each. I was red and green - definitely red anyway. Suddenly she changes the subject round to sex, and I'm blushing like a bull fighter's cape. She says right out,

-Have you ever done it, Ronnie?

Well, its like the surveys they have in Sunday papers where it says, 'Seventy nine percent of fourteen year old boys claim to have had sexual intercourse'. Dead fucking right! They might never have been near a girl, but they'll claim on point of death that they've tommed everything in fucking sight. It makes you wonder about the researchers - don't they think that the 'Six percent of girls that claim to have had sexual intercourse' would have to be working shifts if all the boys were telling the truth? They'd have to do more callouts than the AA to cope.

Anyway, I look at her sheepishly and say,

-Course I fucking have - eleven times!

I'm praying to fuck she won't ask me who with, cos I ain't even kissed any female non-member of me family. But she smiles and says,

-Go on, who with then?

I think fuck this; I'm a year older than her - I'm in fucking charge, so I say,

-No, you tell me who you've been with first.

And she starts reeling them off. This is a thirteen year old flat chested schoolgirl ! Finally she gets to eighth and last and she says,

-And Barry Daniels.

This is music to my ears. I'm thinking if she'll let a tosser like Daniels knob her, she'll definitely let me.

We're lying adjacent to each other but I ain't got a clue what to do next. I certainly don't want to fucking well kiss her. She leans over the Ludo and says deadly seriously,

-Do you want to do it?

-Might as well, I say.

And fuck off to the toilet. When I get there the fucking thing's shrank. I'm stood there looking at it in the mirror, hoping it's at least as big as one of the other eight. I come down five minutes later shaking like a leaf, and she's still on the floor next to the fireplace.

-Nice fireplace, I say.

She tells me her Dad made it. I like it. It's got little individual shelves with diamond shaped mirrors behind them, and a hearth that's made out of wood, with tiles on it. Very neat.

I seen her Dad about six months later. We were both waiting outside the paper shop for the Football Pinks to arrive. He was a big United fan, went to all the home games. They'd drew two all at Leeds that day. I try to be polite, so I remember his fireplace and I say,

-I like your fireplace - it's nice.

The big bastard looks down at me and says,

-You keep away from our house you thieving little bastard, and you leave our Maureen alone.

I'm thinking don't forget the swear box. Funny, the things you remember.

Anyway I finish me beer and I lie down next to her - she's cool as you like and I'm thinking, I wonder if she did it more than the once with any of the eight? She undoes her blouse, which was a waste of time as there was fuck all to see. Then she takes her knickers off. I look the other way while she does it. She lies back and five minutes later she gets the idea that I haven't got an idea. She moves over to me and undoes me trousers. Me one eyed snake is standing to attention, and it's all over in a minute. I've got Gerd Muller's number on me back, I'm number Nine.

Afterwards she poured me another mug of beer to settle me nerves and made me promise not to tell anyone that we'd done it. I promised, then we continued with our game of Ludo. I won with the reds.

The next day I'm first in school, and give everyone who'll listen a match commentary - making sure that the shagging part is extended to make me out to be the Errol Flynn of St Martin's.

Like I say, I pass her on the street regular, and I must have been in a hundred different pubs at the same time as her since, but the last words we spoke to each other was all those years ago, when at five to four she said, 'see you' to me and shouted down the garden,

-Don't tell no-one, Ronnie.

It's a funny thing losing your virginity. It's one of them things you never forget like your first football match. Years later you can still remember every detail. Who was in goal, who was sub, who was Manager. Even the minute the equaliser was scored (If Bolton score first we consider it the equaliser cos sooner or later the other cunts always get one).

SAUSAGE AND EGG

Robbie was really beginning to get on me tits. He had the munchies. So we're stuck in a little cafe next to Victoria station. I've got hold of the baby and the little sod is climbing all over me.

Even though the girl went to pains to explain to Robbie that breakfast ended at eleven, he insists he wants bacon and eggs and not pie and chips. After a long and detailed consultation with the chef she comes back, and says no problem. Time's spinning on and we've only swapped three bags. I just want to get the Kiting started - why can't he have a couple of pies to take out?

I've got a shite of an headache and I'm thinking about having a reverse bowel movement and serenading the toilet bowl. Robbie starts fucking about with his knife and fork; all I can hear is this fucking scraping sound. I ain't gonna ask him to stop. If I do that he'll do it all the more.

-Take their fucking time don't they? he says.

I ain't in the mood for conversation so I just ignore him.

He tries another tack,

-You not hungry then Rooftop?

He ain't gonna leave me alone.

-No, I say - a coffee'll do me.

And I'm praying that the cunt of a waitress will get a move on.

About twenty minutes later the waitress comes over with his order, and it's obvious she's been to a school for the hard of thinking cos she's brought sausage and eggs instead of bacon and eggs. I just know he's gonna start a fucking scene. He takes one look at the plate, stops scraping his knife and fork together and says,

-Hang about love, I ordered bacon, not sausage.

She looks confused, like he's talking a foreign

language.

-What? she says.

Robbie pushes the plate away from him and says,

-Right tent, wrong desert - I want bacon, not sausage.

-Oh, the stupid bitch says and she's about to take it back. I can't believe what I'm fucking seeing. I completely lose the plot and start shouting,

-Eat the fucking sausage, what's it matter? We're in a fucking hurry. It took half an hour for fucking sausage, how long for fucking bacon? Eat will you, for fuck's sake?

Every cunt in the place is looking at me. Robbie, the bastard, is giggling his fucking head off.

-OK, he says smiling, but she ain't getting no tip.

By now I'm as wound up as a clockwork toy on Boxing Day. Robbie turns the screw,

-Have a smoke, he says.

I blank him and he returns to his breakfast, still smiling.

Rory sits patiently sucking at his bottle throughout the tantrum. He's seen it all before - if the little sod had an imaginary bubble of thought coming from his head it would probably say,

-Some fucking family, some fucking life!

Robbie finishes his late breakfast and pushes his plate away. I swig back the remains of me cold coffee as he delves in his pocket for his gear.

-Don't be rolling that shit in here, I say.

Robbie picks up Rory and walks out. I go to pay the bonked out bimbo. She makes a real meal out of the adding up, which is more than the chef did with the sausage and eggs. I can't be bothered waiting for the change so the useless cow gets a good tip.

We walk down to the station and for a change get a bit of fucking luck. There's a train leaving in five minutes and it's the Blackpool one, which is good news cos that means that the first stop is Bolton.

We have a quick visit to Smiths. Robbie buys a *Sun* and has a couple of cans of Coke away. I get meself a *Daily Mirror* and a *Milky Bar* for Rory.

We board the train and get another good bounce of the ball - the fucking thing's empty, so we can spread ourselves out a bit. I'm beginning to cheer up, but as soon as I start to warm to the affair, Robbie pulls out his ganja tin and starts to roll a weed.

-Do you need to? I say.

-Yeah, he replies.

And it's Sid James in *Carry On Regardless.*

The reason I don't like Robbie hammering the stuff is that weed and earners don't mix. That shit breaks down your awareness of everything that's going on around you. Which is probably why people take it in the first fucking place.

Anyway, the train's passing Burnden Park, home of the land's finest under achievers, and heading on into Trinity Street Station. Fuck it, I think to meself, I'll have a quick couple of pints in the town centre; steady me nerves, then it's 'fill your hands with lead you sons of bitches', as Marion Morrison would say.

We have a quick livener to settle our nerves, or at least I do. Robbie and Rory stick to orange juice. It's about twenty past one so we should really be cracking on. I've been on Robbie's back all morning to get a fucking move on, now it's me that's holding the game up.

The trouble is, when it comes to Kiting I've got no fucking bottle, so I need a pint to give me the courage. I've told Robbie that I'm only having the one. But fuck him, I'll neck half of it, get up to go for a piss, and order another on the way back. It'll only take me twenty minutes to down the two, and we can get back to the business of the day.

It's a little shit hole of a pub near Trinity Street Station. It doesn't do a lot in the way of passing trade but the landlord keeps a good pint. I used to drink in it a few years previous when I followed the football regular. I knocked around with a few lads that went for the aggro. I tried not to get involved when it went off, but I've got to admit, I liked the crack when it did.

I got that attitude well and truly knocked out of me though at Chelsea one year. Normally when it went off I was the first one out of it. Which was generally accepted by the other lads - if you got in me way, you got stampeded.

Then this one game we get ambushed, and we're well outnumbered. I do me usual trick of going for reinforcements but it don't work. I get collared down this entry. It's in the middle of some shite hole area I ain't never heard of. All I can say is that if God had heard of it, Sodom and Gomorrah would have got done a day later.

It always gets me that, why do people have such a downer on Sodom? yet no-one remembers Gomorrah. I mean those cunts in Gomorrah were just as bad, but all you ever hear is,

-He was a Sodomite.

Anyway, this fucker comes at me. I'm fucked cos there ain't any of me crew within a hundred yards. I throw up me arms in an act of surrender as he comes forward and say,

-I don't fight. I'm just here for the football. I'm a pacifist.

He keeps moving forward and he's got his hand out. For about thirty pleasing seconds I think he's gonna shake hands. Then he says,

-Peacefully resist this then, Gandhi!

And he slams his fist straight into the side of me face. Like I say, I ain't much of a pugilist, but I knew enough of the rudiments of the art to make me way to the floor, where the cunt delivered a couple of kicks to the head. I don't remember much more.

I wake up and me jaw is well and truly fucked. I had to have it wired up and drink through a straw. A few weeks on the sick paid for by Manchester City Council and a course of Physiotherapy put me right.

The Physiotherapist was a fucking character. One appointment, Dodge drives me down to see him. He starts fucking about with me jaw. It's hurting like fuck.

The Physio says,

-Do you have trouble masticating?

Dodge, who's sat at the other side of a curtain, is pissing his sides laughing.

I'm in fucking agony. The Physio gets hold of me jaw and says,

-Explain to your ignorant friend the difference between masticating and masturbating will you? It might help him get through his Sunday roast faster.

Like I say, the experience sort of put me off being one of the lads and I gave it a miss after that.

Robbie shakes me out of me bout of *All Our Yesterdays* by saying,

-You got stage fright or something, you cunt?

I motion to the bar and say,

-One last one.

I down the dregs and go to the bar and order another. I don't bother getting the boys another orange, they ain't took the top off the first one yet. I get a pint and a small vodka.

Robbie clocks what I do and shouts,

-It's out of your half.

I smile, down it in one, and shout back,

-I got it out of last night's card winnings. Anyway, I should have a fucking expense account.

I've always been a cunt for the drink. It's cost me relationships, jobs, friends - you fucking name it, the drink's cost it. Fuck it though, I wouldn't have it any other way.

I sit back down next to me Comrades in Arms and

slurp at me pint.

The juke-box is playing *Hey Jude* by the Beatles. I hate them Scouse bastards. The only pity about John Lennon getting shot was that it didn't happen at a Beatles re-union and the arsehole that did it didn't get the other three as well.

-Right, says Robbie, down that fucker will you? We can't afford to hang around all day - it's nearly two and you've not Kited a cheque yet. At the rate you do them we'll need to find all-night launderettes.

It's a good one that, for Robbie. He's on form, so I change the subject.

-When's Scots John's car back on the road? I say.

He knows I'm changing the subject, so he gives me a blank.

-Where first? I say.

Robbie shrugs his shoulders, thinks about it, and says,

-We'll both do Chelsea Girl. I'll nip in, get rid of the Swopsie - you can follow thirty seconds later and Kite one.

I nod in agreement, down me pint and fuck off for a piss.

The toilets are like something out of Bleak fucking House. You have to go outside to piss on a slab of fucking slate. I waste as little time as possible. I don't bother washing me hands, the towel looks older than the Shroud of Turin and about as fucking authentic. What was it our Eammon said about religious icons? Oh yeah, if you got together all the pieces of the True Cross from around the world, you'd have enough wood to put a fence round Heaton Park.

I come out and they're up by the door ready to go.

-No time for a last one? I say.

But I'm walking as I say it.

TENNERS

The tenners was a great time while it lasted. Believe it or not, I got involved through this mad Trotsky from the Socialist Workers Party. I don't know how I got to know him, he just sort of appeared on the scene. We called him Groucho - no prizes for guessing why. He kept going on about Marx said this, and Marx said that. He was good for a wind up; he reckoned Marx had an answer for everything. His real name was Richard, and like Big Tony said, you could tell he was a Dick the second he walked through the fucking door. No one took the cunt serious - I always bought the paper off him, but then again I always bought *Watchtower*, and that didn't mean I was a born again anything.

Then this day right out of the blue he comes into the Ram and invites me to go into the toilet with him. I didn't know if he wanted to fight me or fuck me. Anyway, it turns out that he can get hold of as many bent tenners as I can shift. He says he gets them off a comrade at three quid a time. He says he'll put the money up to buy them if I'll exchange them. I tell him I'm game for it, but I'll need me little team with me - Dodge, Big Tony and Norfolk Danny. He says sorted, and starts going on about bringing down the economy of the country. I'm thinking, fuck me; how many does he think the four of us can shift? The daft cunt's up it, but either way if it does harm to the arseholes who run this fucking country, then fuck them. It's got to be more use than Groucho selling *Socialist Worker* to a bunch of drunks who'd rather have a fucking curry than seize the means of production and put them in the hands of the masses.

About a fortnight later and he's in the Ram again, and he signals me into the toilet with a surreptitious nod that the whole pub clocks. He's got a bundle of the fuckers with him. We're in a cubicle and I'm more worried that people are gonna think that I've turned turtle, than up to something. He passes me a couple to inspect; they look the business. Now my natural paranoia starts to work overtime.

-Yeah, I say, they look the part but why do you need me? Why can't you do them yourself?

He looks at me and I can see he's picking his words carefully, and he says,

-I'm not a criminal.

The way he says it ain't demeaning like, but more as if I'm a skilled, time served man. Which I suppose I am.

And that as they say was that. We made an attempt to bring down the economy of the United Kingdom. As usual we gave Manchester a wide berth - borrowed Scots John's van and headed for that friendly gullible arsehole of a place Oldham, where the fast lane is cobbled.

Five of us made the journey. Me, Big Tony, Dodge, Norfolk Danny and Groucho. It was a total no risk operation. Groucho kept all the bent tenners on him. The stupid twat didn't realise he was the canary in our mine. The first sign of any trouble it's all on his fucking toes and he's about as sound as the famous Norwegian Blue. He offered to share them round but Dodge put him straight by saying,

-No Groucho, I've known this crew all me fucking life and I don't trust a one of them. You keep them in your pocket, they're safe there.

Groucho's smiling like Che Guevara in the Bolivian jungle. It don't even enter the silly cunt's head that if we're stopped we don't know him, and all the evidence is in his pocket. Judging from the way he talks it wouldn't need any electrodes to the testicles from the Dirty to obtain a full and frank confession.

It's a fucking doddle - we bounce all round Oldham. Only one tenner at a time, no more. Any problems, which there weren't, and you give it,

-Shit, sorry love, I've just took that as change off that robbing fucking Paki on the market.

Groucho, who's always spouting that all profit is theft, wants five pound back each time we change one to cover whatever. It's only fair I suppose; so it leaves a fiver profit on each one, minus whatever you've spent cashing it.

Big Tony does the first one; gets himself twenty cigs, bungs Groucho a fiver and has enough left for a couple of pints. Dodge does his first one in at a flower stall. He gets a single red rose. I think, creeping bastard wants it for his missus, but he puts it in the first bin we pass. So much for love. I make me debut at a toy stall. I buy a Yo-Yo for sixty pence.

-Sorry love, I've got nothing less, I say.

-No problem, she says.

I'm thinking, there fucking will be when you try to bank it.

Norfolk Danny is like a pig at a trough and keeps wanting to go out of turn.

Right away we've clocked that it's a no lose situation. All the shopkeeper can do is refuse to take it. If you've only got the one on you, even if the Dirty get involved, you could've taken it anywhere. Our gutless Anarchist, who ain't got the bottle to do one himself ain't sussed he's carrying a pocket full of time.

After a morning like kids robbing a toffee shop we adjourn for a liquid lunch. We all take a tenner apiece off the main man and nip in the Tommyfield.

-Don't cash more than one between us in here, we don't want the top dozen tenners in that till having the same fucking number on them, says Tony.

Sound advice, I think, and whip in to get me round in first. That way it ain't costing me fuck all.

Its empty, just a couple of shoppers in. We take a little alcove together out of the way and sit listening to the jukebox. Groucho is all hyped up - he's never been involved with anything like this before and the cunt can't shut up. He's droning on, saying,

-I've got an endless supply. We'll hit every big town in England. Hit the rich bastards where it hurts. Bring the machinery to its knees. It'll be like Germany in the Thirties - inflation will be rampant. Savings will become worthless. It will take thirty pound just to buy a box of matches.

-Not much of a point doing bent tenners when it gets to that fucking stage, says Tony - get some fucking beer in.

Groucho fucks off to the bar. No need to tell him not to use a tenner, the cunt wouldn't have the guts. I'm thinking about all the shit he's just said. It's bollocks - the fat rich people who own everything will always own everything. They've got ninety nine percent of the cake and the rest of us have to scrap for the crumbs. If things started to go like Germany in the Thirties it's the worst off that suffer, or your minorities like the Jews.

Anyway, the cunt comes back with four pints of bitter and a fucking shandy for him.

-I've made a mistake, he says.

We all stare at him. If it's a bad one, there's four men about to defect from the Collyhurst Peoples Army, leaving net membership at one.

-I paid with a twenty and they've give us our tenner back with the change, he says.

We all stare at him and wonder at his fucking stupidity. Then Tony says,

-And you're gonna run the fucking country come the glorious day? Give us the fucker here - I'll get the next round in with it.

The thing with Groucho that I didn't like was that although we were all taking the piss out of him in our little way, I got the feeling he was taking it out of us in a big way. I sometimes caught the devious cunt smirking, and the odd time the Comrade forgot himself and let us know that he was just that little bit brighter than us when it came to anything that really mattered.

The tenners thing came to an head and an end in Blackpool. We went there supposedly for a day but it ended up being three, and although we did in fifteen hundred worth of the tenners, Groucho ended up getting fuck all.

Norfolk Danny drove us down in a borrowed motor. We booked into one of them small boarding houses just off the front. The sort me and Robbie would later tan for tellies and phones. We had a great landlady, the sort that stopped serving when you stopped drinking. Her husband was a little man, about a foot smaller and five stone lighter than her. He spent all his available time out fishing. He used to joke that he had a hospital sick note excusing him sex. He said he had a man that come in and did it for him once a week; the man was expensive, but his wife said he was worth every penny. Judging by the way she carried on I could believe it. She couldn't put a sausage on a plate without making jokes straight out of a fucking *Carry On* film. Out of respect we never Kited any tenners there. Which must have been one of the few places we never.

Right from the start we appalled Groucho with our proletarian behaviour - *Kiss Me Quick* hats, sticks of rock, and that cunt getting his fiver about every third tenner we changed. Even though it was a good earner and we were dependent on him, I'd grown tired of the sanctimonious shithead. When we booked in he insisted he have a single fucking room. No skin off my nose, I jumped in with Dodge, and Big Tony and Danny shared. It was just his attitude, taking it for fucking granted that he was team leader. It also pissed me off that every time he went for a shit or a shower he locked his room and took his key with him. It was as if he didn't trust us. A good job he didn't really, cos we were itching to rob the twat.

Anyway, over the next couple of days we showed him what fucking Anarchy was. We kicked off the first day with a couple of pints in the digs for breakfast. Groucho's wandering round like Sir Alf Ramsey on World Cup Final day, saying shite like,

-Come on lads, ease up on that drink. We've got to get through as many tenners as we can.

As he's giving his speech the landlady, Betty her name was, comes in and clears up the plates.

We all fuck off out and have a morning devaluing the currency. It gets to about one o'clock and we decide to have a fish and chip dinner. It's a gorgeous day so we're all sat outside enjoying the gap in the Ozone Layer. Then I clock what's happening. We've all got a fuck off big plate in front of us and a mug of tea. I look up at Dodge and he's shovelling it down like a practising Catholic the day after Lent. He looks at me, winks and says,

-Remember the Orient Express?

I know he ain't talking about no train or no fucking film, he's talking about a restaurant. The Orient was one of the first Indian restaurants on our side of Manchester. When it first opened me and Dodge had done a runner without paying for our meal. As a consequence, any dubious character eating there afterwards had to pay up front for his scran.

This day in Blackpool we hadn't paid yet, so Dodge's words were obvious to everyone apart from Groucho. I'm looking round the table and we're all stuffing it down like pigs, except Groucho who's silently buttering a slice of bread. Then bam, bam, bam, bam. Four empty chairs as Dodge, me, Danny and Tony give it legs down the street. Groucho's staring after us -ain't got a clue what's happening. Before the stupid bastard can move the owner's got hold of him by the collar and demanding money. The poor cunt has to pay for five dinners, and don't even get a chance to finish his.

When he meets us at the bottom of the street his temper is frayed and he's muttering to himself.

-Bloody idiots. I've got all the tenners on me. I could've been arrested. If you'd have asked I'd have paid, he's saying.

-Yeah, but it's more fun this way, says Tony.

And the tone for the day is set. Blackpool hadn't been hammered at the time so we're hitting everywhere and doing tenners in for fun.

We stop about four and we're all on deckchairs watching the sea.

-Big prawns round here, says Tony.

Danny's eating a big tub of the fuckers.

-The bigger the better, he says.

-Know what they feed on? I say.

-Who the fuck cares? says Danny.

-Shit - they eat shit, says Tony.

-Bollocks, says Danny.

-Yeah, says Dodge - and blood.

Danny's looking dubious, but fuck all is going near his mouth.

-Judging by that one on your fork, it's been sucking on a tampax all fucking morning, says Dodge.

-You must have heard that saying about fat girls - 'Better fed than a Blackpool prawn on a tampax', I say.

And Danny slings his tea.

Groucho's there taking it all in and saying nothing. I've figured out that by now we're working our notice, and that the cunt will sack us when we get back to Manchester. I don't give a fuck cos by now I've decided to rip the cunt off.

I'm lay there, mulling on the best way to do it when Dodge points and says,

-Look at that idiot.

It's no big deal, just some shit for brains with a metal detector who's doing a sort of sweep of the beach looking for whatever. The next thing I know Dodge scuttles behind a wind break.

-Get some change ready, he shouts,

Then he comes out. He's had a shit on his *Daily Mirror*. Groucho's face is a fucking picture,

-Animals, he says and storms off.

Fuck him - miserable bastard!

Dodge puts a load of change in the shit, like raisins in a cake. Folds the paper then trots off to the front about ten yards away from us, and about fifty yards in front of the treasure hunter. Then he opens the paper on what's gonna be supper for the prawns. Digs a hole, puts his shite in it and covers it over. He trots back over to us and we wait.

Ten minutes later the metal detector's bleeping to buggery and its owner thinks he's unravelling Captain Flint's treasure. You should see the cunt's face when he sticks his hand in shit for fifty odd pence. We're all laughing and cheering. But I'll give the cunt his due - he just walks to the front, washes his hand and his findings, and carries on.

-Get more shit on his hands off that sea than he's already got on them, says Tony.

We abandon to the pub. After a couple of pints and a game of pool I say,

-I don't like that cunt.

-Who? they all say.

-Groucho - he's looking down on us, I say.

-Big fucking deal, says Danny; we're all making a butty, so where's the problem ?

But I know I've made me point, and before the next drink is finished we've decided that we're a parachute short, and it's Groucho's. We decide to play his game for a short while. Kite as many tenners as we can. Bung him a fiver each time we Kite one, build the kitty and wait our chance.

The idea how to fuck him was mine. Simple really. We all go out next morning as planned, Kite a few tens then Danny complains he's got the shits,

-One too many Blackpool prawns.

Dodge volunteers to go back with him, and me, Tony and Groucho go about our business. We arrange to meet Dodge in an hour in the Irish Bar. Him and Danny then nip home to get Groucho's spare key off the landlady. All we got to do is keep the Comrade sweet. After a couple of tenners I say to Groucho,

-How many are we doing today pal?

-About sixty, he says.

Miserable twat, I think. Nod appreciatively and say,

-Taking a chance carrying that many aren't you ?

He gives me one of them sneery sort of glances and says,

-Got about twelve on me when we've done these. We can go back for some more.

Stupid cunt - as if twelve is any easier to explain to the Dirty than sixty.

-Great, I say.

And I mean it. Cos by now Danny will have got the spare key from the landlady and him and Dodge will have emptied Groucho's holdall of anything worth having. They'll have packed our belongings, said goodbye to the landlady, and be parked up on Bloomfield Road opposite Blackpool Football Club.

All we have to do is ditch Groucho, which is as easy as it sounds. We get to the Irish Bar, it's a sorted place, a bit expensive, with Bouncers on the door. There's an advertisement in the window saying 'Live music every afternoon featuring Melvin Moonlight and his Moonlight Sonatas'. We nip in for a quick one. As we do so, Melvin's doing his tribute to the King. Before launching his set he tells us that,

-The King was a man I never had the pleasure to meet.

After listening to him butcher a couple of songs, I think to meself that if I owned the bar, the Manager of the local Social Security would be a person that Melvin did get the pleasure to meet.

I get three pints in. We've got to keep the cunt's mind at rest. Big Tony starts on about the revolution.

Tony nods to the bar and says to Groucho,

-See that big long brown thing we passed on the way in? That's called a fucking bar. Get some beer in.

Groucho mutters something and wanders over to the bar as me and Tony wander over to Melvin and out of Groucho's life for good. Melvin's just finished an awful rendition of *Way Down* and I'll tell you, it fucking is on my list. Tony says,

-Do you know *It's Over*?

Melvin curls his lip and says,

-Huh huh.

I bung him a bent tenner and say,

-In five minutes sing it; but before you do, can you dedicate it to a mate of ours called Groucho?

Melvin nods - I've probably doubled his wages. Me and Tony sneak out the door to the strains of *Teddy Bear* - it could've been worse, it could've been *Jailhouse Rock*.

-That tosser couldn't get a fucking standing ovation in a piles clinic, says Tony.

When we get to the car, Dodge and Danny are sat there pissing their sides laughing. I start to get a little bit paranoid that their twenty five percent might be just a little bit bigger than my twenty five percent.

-What's the joke? I say.

Dodge points at Danny and says,

-He's only played hide the Norfolk Sausage with the fucking landlady.

Danny's laughing. Nothing embarrasses that cunt. He shrugs his shoulders and says,

-I had to, she might not have give me the key otherwise.

-Might not? I say - you could've asked her before

you fucked her.
And another earner ended.

CHELSEA GIRL

It's a little bit drizzly. Robbie's in Chelsea Girl doing a Swopsie. I'm out of the way doing a George Formby impression- leaning on a lamp post at the corner of the street (mind you where I come from that means either soliciting or loitering with intent). When Robbie returns, I'll go back and Kite one. The Funny Red Nose wankers are in full swing. Me and Rory have got our smiley face stickers on in case any fucker tries to bleed us for more money. We move to a doorway and watch the world go by.

There's this fat bearded man dressed as a Monk chasing after a couple of schoolgirls. At least I assume they're schoolgirls, could be anything on a day like this. They're giggling and egging him on. I can envisage the headlines in the tabloids when it comes to court:

Monk Defrocks Schoolgirl To Reveal Docker!

No sign of Robbie - he's been gone a fucking age. I take Rory over to a Newsagents to buy him a Milky Bar, and I get caught up on a conversation about charity.

-Champion isn't it? says the newsagent.

He's a bearded, fat man and I wonder if he's related to the monk.

-What? I say, totally indifferent and feigning ignorance.

-How ordinary people will do anything for a laugh as long as some charity benefits.

I'm looking at him and I'm thinking 'stupid bastard'. But what's it matter? If it's gonna make his conscience straight putting a couple of quid in some tin rattled by King Kong then so be it.

-Yeah, I say - heartwarming.

And we're stood there shaking our heads like a couple of nodding dogs in the back of a nineteen sixties Mini Cooper.

He looks at Rory and says,

-He's a little belter, they make it all worthwhile, do the little 'uns.

Again I'm looking at him and again I'm thinking what a load of bollocks. Kids make fuck all worthwhile.

It's like all this shite put about by tosspots who say that the greatest thing they've ever seen is a child being born. Like fuck it is. Anyone who really believes that wants to get out more often, watch a bit of horse racing, or take in the odd film. I've seen babies be born, and it's screaming and swearing, loony midwives, and buckets of blood.

On Rory I had this mad Irish nurse shouting...

-Look at the business end, father!

I thought, like fuck I will. Then she grabs me, spins me round and I'm staring at the most terrifying sight I've ever seen. I'm looking at it and I think to meself, me knob ain't going up there again. I start to want to heave. So I turn and run. Fuck this for a game of soldiers. All I can hear behind me is Florence O' Nightingale shouting,

-You're a coward, father! A coward is what you are!

Father was the right word, cos I was moving like a Catholic Bishop out of a raided brothel.

I get outside Crumpsall Hospital and it's two-thirty in the fucking morning. I can't even get a drink. Eleven hours of labour and she gives birth when the pubs are shut.

It's the beginning of the end that, having kids - that's when they've got you nailed down. That's when you find out who really is the fucking boss. When you're on your own and skint it don't really matter. When you're stuck in a fucking terrace with a mortgage and kids, and it's coming up to Christmas; that's when you're up against it.

Mr Newsagent is stood waiting for a suitable reply.

-Yeah, I say, they make everything worthwhile.

I turn and walk out of the shop.

I see Robbie coming round the corner.

-Took your fucking time, I say.

He just shrugs and shows me the money.

-Any problems? I say.

-No, he says.

I empty me pockets, give it all to him apart from a bit of loose change. That way if it comes on top they get back as little as possible. I know it's only a fucking precaution, but it seems a bit defeatist to me. All told we've got two hundred and odd now. Not bad for half a day's work.

Time now to build up the bags for tomorrow's Swopsies. This time I'd insist Clarissa or Margery did them in. I mean, no use having a dog and barking yourself. Kiting and Swopping on the same day is a real fucking ball ache. Talk about pass the fucking parcel. One minute I've got Rory, the cash, the remainder of yesterday's bags and today's bags while Robbie swops one. Then he's got today's bags, the cash and yesterday's bags while I Kite one.

-Is it crowded? I ask.

-Not really, just two old fuckers looking at skirts, he answers.

-What are the assistants like? I ask out of professional curiosity.

-Two of 'em. One aged about nineteen, chubby with big tits who does all the talking. The other, same age; scrawny, tall with no tits, who does all the listening. Scrawny's got a right fucking snotter on her - must've told more lies than Pinnochio.

I nod. I've already decided Big Tits is having me business. It's nothing to do with her mammary glands, but something I've learned in life is people who talk too much pay fuck all attention to anyone else.

We walk down to the corner - it's getting crowded in the Town Centre now. He's got a weed out. Fuck me, I don't need this. It's bad enough getting through the day without the additional worry of me fucking partner getting nicked for being in possession of an illegal substance. I motion to a pub and say,

-I'll meet you outside there in ten minutes, and don't smoke anymore of that shit.

-Fuck you, he says, I'll stop smoking this stuff when you stop drinking.

We separate and I'm thinking I'd sack the bastard if he wasn't so fucking good at his part, and I wasn't so fucking bad at mine.

I walk into Chelsea Girl; there's three customers and two assistants. They're the two Robbie described, and he'd read them like a book. I was at the door and all I could hear was Big Tits' voice. It's as if she's being sponsored to use the name Brian the most times in a limited period, cos that's all I could fucking hear, Brian this and Brian that. Still, if it made my errand a little easier, good old Brian.

I do me concerned Daddy routine and usher Rory round the clothes. Giving out a load of shite as I go.

-Would Mummy look nice in this?

and,

-Oh no, not her size.

Rory's staring at me, happy to be playing Sid Little to my Eddie Large. God, the kid needs a new role model. We're about five yards from the counter, looking at a rack of coats. Big Tits and Scrawny are debating boyfriends. Well, not really debating cos Scrawny can't get a word in.

I give it about five minutes of fucking about and I walk up to the counter holding Rory. I put him down next to the till. There's a collection box on it so I sling a few coppers in it and say,

-Can I take a sticker for the baby?

Big Tits waves a hand and carries on chatting. I find meself staring at her breasts and listening to all her shite. She's saying,

-So I said to Brian, it's either Debbie or me. Make your mind up but don't expect me to wait forever.

As she's saying this I'm weighing her tits up, and thinking he'd have to be stupid to pick Debbie. There's no let up, she just won't fucking shut up.

-I said, I'm not waiting around forever. What's she got that I haven't?

I stop looking at her tits and stare at her mouth. It's the sort of gob that could suck twenty pences out of a parking meter.

Suddenly she shuts up and turns round, looks at me and says,

-Yes?

It takes me aback, I wasn't expecting her to finish so quick. I look at the cow and I start to hate her. I've become a Debbie man - I hope Brian's run off with her.

-Sorry? I say.

-What? she says.

And I start thinking that she must have a bucket of men's bollocks under her bed at home, that's she's ripped off without anaesthetic, and now she's after mine.

I place the coat neatly on the counter and say,

-Can I have this please?

She looks at the tag. Starts slowly packing it away and says very curtly,

-Forty-two pounds fifty please.

A bit of a low price really, considering I'll be doing the Swopsie with it. I should've slung a couple of bras in as well to get it as near to the fifty quid as possible. But I'd feel a right cunt buying a bra. So I leave it even though Robbie will give me grief.

I take out me wallet. Well, when I say my wallet, it ain't really - it's one Robbie got while out Mooching. It looks the part - pure leather. Rory's climbing all over me. Perfect, I think. I do the signature; it's not perfect, but it ain't that bad. I pass her the cheque and the guarantee card. She looks at them, deliberates, then passes them to Scrawny. I'm beginning to think that Big Tits' surname is fucking Sondheim, cos she makes a song and dance about everything.

-Get Maureen, she says.

I stay cool. I know the book's new. No time now for panic. Besides, three women, empty shop, no sign of Security.

And I remember me and Clarissa in Stolen from Ivor's in Middleton a couple of month before.

It was a similar situation, Clarissa does the signature gets it spot on, but the girl goes out back to check something. She's got the card with her and she's gone an age. I look through and see her on the phone doing a lot of gesticulating and suddenly I'm doing a *don't panic Mr Mainwaring*.

-Pick up the fucking baby, I say to Clarissa, leave the buggy here. You do a right and I'll meet you behind the Old Roebuck.

I'm just about to run when Clarissa grabs me arm.

-Calm fucking down, she says, stop panicking.

Me head's in bits.

-She's on the blower to the fucking Dirty, I'm saying through gritted teeth.

I try to pull away but she won't let me.

-Listen tosspot, Clarissa says annoyed to fuck- she answered the cunting phone and the Dirty don't ring round on spec. It's a fucking customer so you shut the fuck up and wait.

I'm stopped in me tracks.

-Any more hysterics and you get a slap like they do on the films, she says. Then she smiles and adds, -Miles Platting wide boys I've shit 'em.

Anyway about two minutes and major palpitations later Maureen comes out. Big Tits motions to me and gives Maureen the card and cheque. She pulls a face like someone being buggered by a Rhinoceros, then she takes a list out. It's every Kiter's nightmare - it's the Stolen Cheque List, and she's thumbing through it. I know the book came from Doncaster two days ago and I know it ain't on her fucking list. I'm as waterproof as a fish's head but I feel about as safe as a pillion rider on the wall of death. What I don't need is this Maureen bitch to take it personal and start ringing banks. What I've got to do is be polite but firm. Me kid needs feeding; I'm meeting his Mother in twenty minutes. Maureen's thumbing through the list.

Once she's past page one it's a useless exercise, so I say,

-Any problems love?

She smiles a smile and says,

-Just routine.

And I'm thinking if that was genuinely my cheque card she's fucking about with, I'd give these three useless fucking tosspots a right arse kicking.

I'm just about to use the 'baby is hungry' routine when Maureen passes the card back to Big Tits and says,

-No, it's clear.

Big Tits parcels up the coat. As she's doing so, she starts up her conversation again with Scrawny. This really pisses me off. I had her down as a soft touch and she's given me five minutes of grief.

Oh well, I think, you've had your fun, I'm gonna have mine. She passes me the bag without turning. So I wait till she does. Scrawny nods to her and she turns,

-Yes? she says.

I look her in the eye and say,

-If I'm any judge of men, your Brian will be knocking the back out of Debbie as we speak.

Me and Rory turn to walk out, and I can hear Scrawny laughing.

It just goes to show how you can misjudge people. When I walked in that shop I thought she'd be easy pickings. I read her fucking character wrong. That reminds me of a twat that used to drink in the Ram a few year ago. Wally was his name, and on the face of it you couldn't meet a nicer man. If you were a bit skint he'd buy you a pint or lend you a couple of bob. He'd always treat you to a game of pool. In short, he was a proper fucking gent. About fifteen years older than us, a sorted man. Like fuck he was. One night we're in the Ram and the place is chocker. This young kid walks in, taps Wally on the shoulder. Wally turns round and the kid butts him in the nose.

The fucking pub erupts - every cunt wants to hit the little twat. Wally's on the floor. The claret's everywhere and his nose is busted to fuck. Sellotape's got a sort of Half Nelson on the kid. Someone smacks him with a pool cue. The next thing I know he's bundled into the toilet and he's gonna be lynched. Albert the landlord is trying to break it up, he don't want murder on his premises. The kid's bleeding but he ain't backing down, and he ain't fucking scared. Albert's in front of him keeping us off. I'm a fucking pacifist who can't fight, but I want to hurt him bad.

Albert backs the kid into a cubicle and says,

-Why'd you do it, you fucking shithouse?

The kid's maybe sixteen. I ain't never seen him before. He looks at Albert and says,

-He's me Dad.

There's a stunned silence. Then the kids adds,

-You bunch of wankers, you think you fucking know him! You think he's fucking great! He licks arses in here, buys your beer, then he comes home and batters me, me Mam and me sister!

As he's saying it he's crying.

-He puts cigarettes out on me Mam's arm for fucking fun! He makes us kids stand facing the wall for hours! You think you fucking know him? The cunt won't come home till he's spent his wages on beer with you!

185

I want to walk out. I don't want to hear it. I like Wally, he's one of us. But I'm rooted to the spot. I have to listen. The kid's sobbing now,

-I've been hit with fists, sticks, bats! You fucking name it! Have any of you ever seen your little sister butted? You fucking wankers!

I just put down the pool cue I'm holding and walk out of the toilet. Wally's on a chair - a couple of lads are round him.

-Get us a drink, he's saying.

A voice behind me says,

-Fuck you.

I turn and it's Albert the landlord.

Like the kid said that day, I'm a wanker when it comes to judging character.

TWO FAT LADIES

The Lone Ranger and Tonto adjourn for a late lunch. We pick a nice little pub in the town. There's a few shoppers in, some workers and some Funny Red Nosers. The tension between me and Robbie is pretty good now. I've flirted four cheques, all for good amounts, and there's only four left in the book.

We're both sat there having a Hollands' meat pie and a pint of bitter. Rory's got an orange juice - each to his own.

-Listen, says Robbie, let's do another two then we quit. I'll go Mooching tomorrow. Clarissa and Margery can do the Swopsies and you can Kite the last two on the market. Me and Clarissa need some paint and stuff, so get us that and you do in the other on whatever you need.

This is music to me fucking ears. I think, get this pint down me, half an hour's worth of fucking about, and we're on our way home. The real bonus for me though is being allowed to Kite the last couple on a market. It's Robbie's book, so he dictates where it's worked. The Swopsie's great because it's pure money, and a book done in well will bring in over a grand. But you can only do the main stores that have more than one branch. On a market you have to keep what you Kite, but there's no pressure. If you've got a card and a book, in the main a stall holder don't give a fuck cos he's covered. Even if he don't like the look of your signature he ain't gonna shut up shop and hang around a Police Station with you all day. A lot of stall holders buy bent gear so they'll take bent cheques, no problem.

So I'm made up; I'm planning to get me and Margery a pair of jeans and a bit of something for the kids - that way I'm back in her good books.

-Cheers Robbie, I say.

And I'm starting to like the bastard again.

If I had me way I'd do nothing but markets, and flog the stuff pub to pub. I wouldn't make a quarter of the money but it would keep me from an early fucking grave.

The pub's half full now. Robbie slings some music on. It's pretty lively stuff, but not the kind of shit I like.

I shout over to him,

-It's coming out of your half.

A couple of shopgirls come over and sit near us. You know the kind of thing, near enough to show an interest but not near enough to look too interested.

We get chatting - they've finished work early. Robbie asks them what they do. I don't know if it's out of professional interest or he's just being a nosy cunt. They say they're part-time at somewhere called Warners. It's no fucking use to us cos it's a little shop and you can't do Swopsies there. They're both bang into music and take the piss out of Robbie's choice. Robbie's hammered on the weed and enjoying the banter. I'm just concentrating on staying this side of sober till the last two cheques are done in.

They all start playing Twenty fucking Questions, asking each other stupid fucking music trivia. They're younger than me so I ain't got a fucking clue what the fuck they're on about. I don't give a shit anyway, I'm a Bob Dylan fan, and if Bob didn't write it then I don't fucking sing it.

I sit back listening - the fattest one has got Robbie stumped. She's made up, I think she's gonna have an orgasm with all the excitement,

-Go on, she says, what's Captain Sensible's real name?

Robbie considers himself an expert on music, so it's a matter of personal pride that he gets it right. He's racking his brains. Not a lot of racking there, I'm thinking.

-I know it, he says, it's on the tip of me tongue.

I start laughing and say,

-The only thing that's ever been on the tip of your tongue is a woman's clitoris.

The shopgirls giggle and they carry on with their limited version of Mastermind.

I'm left weighing them up and wondering what they'd be like in the sack. I mean you never can fucking tell can you? Just cos they look like they should be working on the Burmese railway dragging logs and dodging tusk hunters don't mean a thing. Take Margery. She's a good looking girl and I love her to bits but I could handle a little more enthusiasm in bed. Sometimes when we're on the job I feel like slapping her to make sure she's still conscious.

No, it's like Amy used to say,

-Only one way to tell on the shagging front and that's to take a suck it and see type of approach.

I lose interest and survey the crowd in the pub. It's a cosmopolitan crew, mainly due to Funny Red Nose day. As I look round I can see Belly Dancers, American Footballers and even an Adolf Hitler impersonator. Now he's a fucking character; he's well pissed and speaks in a broad Lancashire accent. He insists on saying, *Achtung Jukebox!* every time he passes the fucker, which is roughly four times a minute. His routine goes on for twenty minutes and includes such gems as,

-Give us another one of them Deutschland Uber Ales.

And,

-If I come back it will be no more Mr Nice Guy!

It's obvious the sad bastard has been practising his routine since the last Red Nose Day. I leave Robbie and the girls in deep debate about Paul Weller. I grab hold of Rory, and in the words of many a racing commentator 'I approach the penultimate fence'. We've already got four bags and a baby to carry, so I want to Kite this one for something small. I'm passing Argos, so I stroll in; the beer has given me courage, I'm moving like shit off a shiny shovel.

I flick through the catalogue till I find what I'm looking for. Most people shop for a particular item, a good Kiter shops for a price. As near to fifty pound as fucking possible. I spot a ring at forty nine pound ninety nine. Fuck them, they can keep the extra penny.

I pick up Rory and we go over to where the till is. I've filled the little chitty thing out. The girl on the till is as ugly as fuck, as busy as fuck, and as indifferent as fuck. I love her at first sight. This must be the Klondike cos I've struck gold. I write the cheque out, pass her the card and cheque and she looks at it with all the care and attention that Mr Pastry with a hangover would put into decorating his mother-in-law's house.

-Busy day? I say.

She don't say anything, she just makes a face. It's as if she's attempting to get each corner of her mouth to touch the outside of each eye simultaneously. Never mind love, I think to meself, you're on me Christmas Card list. I'm fucking Group Captain Biggles now cos I'm flying over to where you pick the goods up. I hand over me receipt and wait about two minutes. A young kid opens the package, shows me a ring (the one I ordered, not his). I nod yes and I'm on me way back out the door. Robbie won't even have noticed I've gone. Sell me clothes, I'm going to Heaven!

Meanwhile back at the Ranch the pub's become hammered with more people finishing work. Robbie's still sat with the bags, both kinds; our shopping and the two music lovers. I sit Rory down and get the drinks in. A pint of orange, a pint of bitter and a double vodka and Coke. I bring them over and plonk them on our table. The girls look at the drinks and think one of them has been left out. Well they're wrong, they've both been left out. I neck the vodka, pass Robbie the orange and place the bitter in front of me. I'm feeling the drink a bit now.

-Where the fuck you bin? says Robbie.

The two girls get up to go. They've wasted half an hour and ain't even been bought a drink. It's their own fault for being fat. You can't have the last cream cake and still have men whistling at you.

-See you, says the fattest one to Robbie.

He looks at her and shouts her back. She's eager to find out what he wants. She sits down next to him smiling.

-You don't sweat much for a fat girl do you? he says.

She gets up swearing.

I'm laughing me balls off - it don't pay to beat Robbie at music questions.

He asks me again.

-Where the fuck you bin?

I smile and pass him the ring. He looks at it, clocks the receipt, and for once I get what could be considered a fucking compliment,

-Nice one, he says. You should kick the day off half pissed, then we wouldn't waste most of the fucker. .

Cheeky bastard, I think.

-And you should try getting out of your fucking pit in the mornings.

We settle down for half an hour's rest. Rory's already got his head down and the little sod's snoring.

Most babies dream about their mothers or having a bottle. He's probably dreaming that he's up on some roof with a gun shouting, *You'll never take me alive, Copper!* We have a couple more, then fuck off when Adolf starts his routine again.

GOD'S DAY

Our Eammon's got this belief, fuck knows where he got it from,he's a big fucking reader so it could be anywhere, the Koran or last week's *101 Ways To Start A Fight* . What he reckons is that when you die, you go to Heaven, everyone goes to Heaven, otherwise it ain't fair. Which is right if you think about it. I mean if Sister Theresa would've had the same bounce of the ball as Myra Hindley, who's to fucking say what would've happened? Plus a lot of it's genetics - if your old man was a loud mouth pisshead, 6/4 on you'll become one as well. So one way or the fucking other it's out of your hands.

Anyway you die, I think we can all take that as read, and you're put in a waiting room with every other cunt that died on the same day (you take a number like at the Social and you sit down). Sooner or later God gets around to you. Imagine the sort of thing, a celestial debriefing, St Peter gives you a tick sheet. You know, like you see in *Woman's Own*, put an X in the box of your preference:

	BAD	POOR	OK	GOOD	FUCK OFF	BRILLIANT
CHILDHOOD						X
PUBERTY					X	
YOUTH				X		
MIDDLE AGE		X				
OLD AGE	X					

Then before you get eternal happiness with everyone you've ever loved, God says,

-OK son, your best day, any one from birth to death, you get to live over from midnight to midnight as a reward for being part of the experiment. Go on, our kid (God's a Miles Platting boy), which fucking one? But remember, you get to change nothing.

I love that thought and I hope to fuck it's true.

I even know what me day of days would be as well. Fuck all to do with thieving, cheating, lying and gambling. It was this one beautiful day I lived back before all the stars got tore down.

Margery was heavily pregnant on our first, little Brendan, she was still at her Mam's cos I was struggling to get a mortgage together. Trouble was I had County Court judgements against me for fraud. So I had to raise a deposit and use bent documentation. She's getting more and more pregnant and things are getting more and more pressing, or depressing. For the fucking life of me I didn't know how I was gonna afford it all and I was doing me bollocks in at the bookies on a daily basis. (Margery would've known how hard I was trying for her if she would've known how much I was losing). This one day I get three doubles and a treble up on the dogs and I'm £169 in front. She's been going on about a pram and carry cot for the imminent arrival so I go round to her Mam's on Collyhurst. God, talk about Bleak House, they had fuck all. I'm half pissed and I make her this promise that the next day I'm gonna call for her and take her to buy this blue cord pram thing that she's seen on Oldham Street.

Next morning I'm up and ready for work when the phone goes.

-Don't go into work, Ronnie. Remember we've got to get that pram for the baby today.

And that was it - I need two snookers and all the colours to get out of this fucker.

And thus began God's day. I took Margery shopping and fucked work off. We get to Oldham Street and all I'm thinking about is get the mission aborted and get in the pub and get things sorted. But no fucking chance - she's set her mind on making a day of it and worse still she's set her heart on the blue cord fucker. Which is out of me price range if I'm gonna have enough left over for a piss-up and another attempt at kicking Mr Ladbroke's arse.

I say,

-Let's think it over, while we have a quick one in the Kings.

We're sat in the corner. I've got two pints in for me and an orange juice for Margery. I'm just taking the top off me first when she takes me right out of me stride.

-I love you, Ronnie, she says.

Fuck me, I think tactics - she's after that blue cord fucker.

-Love you too sweetheart, I reply trying to buy time, got to think of some excuse why the red one at twenty-five quid cheaper is the model we'll be road testing in Newton Heath.

We know it's a boy cos she's had one of them scan things. Spoils it a bit that, knowing what it's gonna be before it's been born. A bit like opening your Christmas presents early or knowing the result of Match of the Day before you turn the box on.

She's sat there staring at me and honest, she looks just like a little furry fucking animal trapped in a waste paper basket. Soft green eyes, strawberry blonde hair cut in a bob and mandatory pink smock.

-You're the only person that's ever been nice to me, she says, and gets hold of me hand.

Now let me tell you something: if any person of the opposite sex ever says that to you there's only one thing to do - put your fucking pint down and get out of where you are as fast as fuck and if someone of the same sex says it to you, make a mental note not to go back to their flat with a carry-out.

I don't know where the fuck this conversation is leading but I know it's being taken out of me hands.

I take a good swig of me pint. Last night's beer must be getting to me cos I find meself saying,

194

-It's only fucking money, fuck it, there's only one pram for us, kid ..... the blue cord one!

And she fucking hugs me right in front of every cunt. I fucking hate it when some twat shows me real emotion cos you just know sooner or later you're gonna shit on them and that's the thing you're gonna remember while you're doing it.

So we buy the blue cord fucker and I'm left with about twenty-three fucking pound which means it's fast approaching ditching time for Margery.

-Can we push it home, Ronnie? she says.

Like fuck, I'm thinking, do I look like a candidate for some home for the barking mad?

-No sweetheart, I say, first time anyone pushes that it has to have our baby in it.

Anyway we start to walk home and we get near Granelli's and it starts raining so we trot down to Butler Street and jump in the Angel.

It's empty, just the way I like it, so we sit down in the vault, alone apart from old Joey.

Joey's a radgepot but he's an harmless old cunt really, a sort of ghost of all Margery's Christmases to come. The second he sees us he starts. Me and Margery are wearing these identical blue and yellow Makita coats that I did a possession is nine tenths with from work. This gives him his ammunition.

-Hans and fucking Hermann, the German bob sleigh team! he shouts - where's the fucking sledge? If you've left the cunt outside it'll be on bricks by now.

-Get back on the piste, you old twat, is me witty re-joiner.

Which starts the mad bastard on a tirade of abuse based around a Winter Sports theme that only someone with a fully paid up subscription to Radio fucking Mars could possibly understand. As he sits down he finishes with the mind bending,

-If you see a tobogganist get us ten Woodbine and a

rough shag.

This tickles Margery, she's having the time of her life. A new pram and meeting Rooftop's quality friends all on the same day.

We sit there, nothing to say. It's funny, right the way through our relationship, the good times the bad times, no matter how pregnant she was, I couldn't look at Margery without wanting to fuck her. Fuck it, I think, ego massage time. I mean let's have it fucking right, I'd just spent me gambling money on a pram. Least she can do is let me bask in the glory.

-Why'd you love me? I say, hoping that even if she don't say I'm great in bed she might say I'm halfway decent on a fireside rug.

She stops sudden, hesitates, then says,

-You don't hit me.

Fuck me, I'm thinking, is that the sum total of me pulling power?

Then for the first time ever she starts to tell me about her life and it wasn't fucking pleasant I can tell you.

-They all fucking hit me, hit me or ignored me, every fucking one of them. No matter what, no matter how hard I tried, they hit me or hurt me.

I'm gob smacked but for once I keep me gob shut.

-You know what my first memory of life was? Being locked in a fucking cupboard, that's what. I'd wet the bed and that bastard Tom Welsh locked me in a cupboard with a boiler in it. Let me out two hours later stinking of me own piss then sent me to school. The more I pissed the bed the more he hit me and the more he hit me the more I pissed the bed.

Shit, I'm thinking, I don't need to hear all this. Can't she just say she loves me cos I've got a nice bum or something? But it's like she's trying to purge her soul, some kind of reverse confession, I've got her pregnant so I deserve some sort of explanation for the person that she is.

-Three fucking months, day in day out, he locked me in that cupboard.

Then she cracks what I presume to be a joke though I've never felt less like laughing in me whole fucking life.

-It got so that I thought the mop was some sort of relative, she says.

And there was a stunned silence. I've spent me whole life being a fucking smart arse. I'm known for it. No situation leaves me short on the cynicism front. But I honestly just want to put me arms round the kid and make everything all right. As if you can put a plaster on a bleeding artery.

-Listen, I say (sorry that I started all this shite), I'll never hurt you for anything.

She smiles and I head for the bar. I count what I've got left, no chance of an all dayer, so I get shorts in. I get meself a pint and a vodka, Margery a brandy and lemonade and Joey a Bells whisky.

Joey clocks me approaching. I put the whisky down, he slings it back in one and shouts,

-Sex, Drugs and Rock and Roll! No sex, no drugs and I hate that cunt Presley!

I sit back down next to Margery and before she can say anything, I say to her,

-Listen babe, get that down you, girl. Everything that is past is history. All that matters is today.

Then I quote her something I once seen in a Christmas cracker - Today is a gift, I say, - that's why they call it the present.

She don't want the brandy but I force her to drink it, tell her it's medicinal and in a way I suppose it is.

While she's drinking it I go to look at the weather. It's Manchester so why should I be surprised that it's pissing it down. I go back over to her, she seems calmer now.

-I do love you Ronnie, she says, and I look at her

face and I know that she means it.

Then she starts to tell me what 'crime and punishment' meant in her world. Fuck it, I'm thinking, punishment in our house was not getting a piece of me Mam's home made coconut cake on a Sunday morning if you'd done something wrong during the week.

She told me how Robbie was sent out to steal their dinner at the age of seven. There wasn't any food in, so no fucking hassle, send the heir to the throne out to do an Oliver. Robbie knew before he was primary school age that there was fuck all the Dirties could do to him. Trouble was he ended up in institution after institution. It sort of put mine and Robbie's nefariousness into perspective - I was playing games and that poor cunt was surviving.

She told me how Tom Welsh used to make her sister Beryl repeat over and over 'I'm so ugly no man will ever want me'. With such great effect that for the next twenty years she apologised every time some twat stood on her toe.

I sat and listened to the catalogue of atrocity for over an hour and I've never felt so helpless, yet so close to another human being. That afternoon you couldn't have put a Rizla paper between us we were that close.

She finishes off telling me about her classmates singing songs to her,

-I used to dread first fucking play, she said, they'd all be waiting. Marina Burrows and her arse licking mates. With their Wendy fucking houses and Brownie fucking uniforms. I'd try and hide down by the netball courts but they always found me. Then it would start.

She starts singing and her words cut through the air like a hot razor blade through weed.

-I know a girl have you met her?...

Margery, Margery the bed wetter.

As she gets to this point tears are rolling down her face and I do the nicest thing I've ever done in me life.

I kiss away the tears. Thank fuck the pubs empty.

-Fuck Margery, I say and there's a lump in me throat.

-I just w-w-want you an-d the baby, she's trying to say.

I put me arms round her and cuddle her. Hold her tight. She's so warm, so open, so raw and so hurt. I wish I could hold her like this forever. Stop every bad arrow the crossbow of life fires at her. But I can't.

Joey clocks what's happening and goes into song mode.

-*Tears for souvenirs is all I have*, he starts singing and he gives as good a rendition as the old Tax Dodger ever did. It has the effect Joey intended, it makes me and Margery laugh.

We sit there holding hands. I don't know what to fucking say. I'm glad I fucked work off.

I get the beer in again, bitter and vodka for me, half a lager for Margery and fuck all for Joey (wouldn't want to fuck the old chirper's vocal chords up).

-Everything OK? Dreary Donna the barmaid asks.

-Yeah, I say, she's just a bit weepy, be the baby I suppose.

-You look a bit weepy yourself Rooftop, your hay fever coming on or what? she says smiling and walks off.

I look out the door - the rain's got a little easier.

-Wanna risk it? I say.

Me and Margery finish our drink and prepare to face a rainy Miles Platting afternoon that I'd give it all just to live again.

-Come on girl, I say, let's get you home.

And we walk up Oldham Road splashing each other in puddles, kicking rain over each other and playing ticky-it. What did some fucking psychiatrist say ? 'Love, the only socially acceptable form of insanity'.

We get back to Bleak House. Her mam Alice is sat there watching some soap. I'm dying for a shag so I do a quick audit of the International Gold Reserves. I've got enough left to buy half a bottle of vodka and treat Alice to a game of Bingo. So it's hero time.

-Get your hair done, Alice, I've got your Bingo money, I say.

I always liked Alice. I knew her way before I'd ever heard of Margery. Years earlier we'd had a quiz team from the Heywood Arms and Alice used to read out the questions at the home games. She was sorted at it apart from small anomalies like pronouncing Hypnotherapist as Hypno the rapist but hey, even George Best once missed a penalty.

We were the league's whipping boys but we always had a laugh. You know the sort of thing,

-Who led the Israelites after Moses ?

-Desmond fucking Dekker.

-Who died and was brought back to life ?

-Marty cunting Hopkirk.

And so fucking forth.

Anyway, I got on well with Alice so she had no problem with me fucking her daughter and even less when I got Margery pregnant and didn't do a Captain Oates. Funny thing, Margery had hero worshipped me without me even knowing it. In fact I didn't even know the poor cunt existed. She told me about one time she was sat on the Heywood step watching me with Dee. She said that every time I kissed Dee she wished it was her.

I said,

-I don't think Dee went in for that lesbian stuff.

Her Mam fucks off to Bingo and it's eyes down for rumpy-pumpy, but before you can say six and nine-sixty nine she decides she's fucking hungry.

She starts cooking this curry shite out of a packet and I'm quite hungry meself. She dishes it up and I decide to have a cheese butty instead (I'll tell you, if Oliver Twist would've tasted Margery's cooking he'd have asked for fucking less).

I whip out to the shops for the vodka and walk back in a steady drizzle.

-Fuck, I say when I get back, - it's pissing it down. Thought it was never gonna fucking let up.

She's got a cheap bottle of coke with about as much fizz in it as Manchester City and I pour me first vodka, borrowing some of it. We sit there watching Bruce cunting Forsythe and I get meself anaesthetised. About an hour later I'm all over her like Germany against San Marino and we go up to do the dirty deed.

Her bedroom was a fucking classic, more furniture in an Albanian soup kitchen - just an old wardrobe and a single bed with a quilt. Normally we could have shagged to Rossini's *The William Tell Overture* we went at it that fast. But today was different - after all she'd said, I just wanted to be tender and gentle.

-Fuck me, she says, you been on the weed or what?

And we both hold each other laughing.

She falls asleep afterwards curled up next to me and I know that for the first time ever we've made love. I know that all the rest that went before was just sex and that something some fucking where that I can't quite put me fucking finger on had changed. I look down at this beautiful seven month pregnant teenager and I know that this is the zenith and that there are a whole lot of different nadirs out there, ready, willing and fucking able to crush me.

And years later when she dropped me like a vase from a verandah, the part that really hurt the most was when she likened me to Tom Welsh.

-He had more guts than you, she said, at least he did it with his fists so you could see it coming. At least he never pretended to fucking love. Never told you things to build you up just so ten minutes later he could make you feel like the shit beneath his shoe. You, you no good wanker, you cut me to pieces with words and sneers and mental fucking torture.

I'm stood crying at the other end of the phone.

-You know what love is? she said, -love is when there's millions of fucking lights on in your body and they're all shining for one fucking person. I had millions of lights shining for you, you no good twat.

As she's saying it she starts crying.

-But light by fucking light you put them all fucking out. Every time you talked down to me, every time you fell down drunk on the kitchen floor, every time you never came fucking home another light went out. Till in the end there wasn't a light in my body left on.

She pauses.

-But I love you, I say.

-Yeah well I don't fucking love you, she says. Right the way through I wasn't allowed a fucking opinion, couldn't open me fucking mouth.

I'm hurt and I've gotta hurt back.

-Couldn't open your fucking mouth? I say - the only time you kept the cunting thing shut was when I asked for a fucking gobble. Listen, you bitch, I should've left you in that cupboard and married the fucking mop.

And there was silence on the other end and we never spoke again.

But that was years later.

And anyway I'll tell you what, despite it all when God says,

-Go on kid, any one day.

I'm gonna be heading down Oldham street with a little angel in a pink smock and we're gonna be buying that blue cord pram all over again.

YUNKA

We leave the pub and we're in the street. The drizzle's started again, which has one good side effect - it keeps the Red Nosers down to the bare minimum. I'm feeling half pissed now and Rory's getting heavy. He's hardly had fuck all to eat all day. This is the last one and then we abandon ship.

I look at Robbie - the twat's smiling. He's had that much weed that his mind has rented a flat in Cuckoo Land.

-Thank fuck this is the last one, I say.

-Do here, Robbie says.

We're outside Marks and Spencers.

-No, I say, didn't Scots John say something about Marks?

-What's that Scots cunt know? he says.

I'm racking me brains trying to think what he said, but I can't. Too much fucking beer and vodka have clouded the airwaves.

Rory starts crying. I ask Robbie for the tub of mush I made in the morning. It's cold now, but it's OK. We go in a doorway and sit the little fella on a ledge. His eyes light up when he sees his scran, and he hammers it down. It's obviously what he needs cos he perks up right away.

Robbie says,

-Will you fucking look at that?

I look up and some cunt is doing a Gene Kelly. He's got an umbrella and he's *Singing In The Rain*. As usual, it's for fucking charity.

-What's he on? Robbie says.

I finish feeding Rory and use me hankie to wipe his mouth. Then I give him a bit of his orange drink to wash it down. He smiles. I check him - he's still dry, which is a good job cos I only brought the one disposable with me and I had to use that in the pub near the station. Robbie's moaning cos I didn't go to the toilet to change the kid. Fuck that - I ain't putting my lads' arse on no cold floor for no fucker. I take Rory's dummy out, clean it and give it to him. He sits on his ledge contented. He'll probably grow up knowing more about the shooting in the Blind Beggar by the Krays than the healing of the Blind Beggar by Christ- but what the fuck.

Me and Robbie look out at the diminishing crowd. It's getting on for half five - tea time, the fuckers will be off home. It's raining heavy now. A Hare Krishna conga line dances by.

Robbie points at Marks and says,

-Are we doing here or not?

-Yeah OK, but give it five minutes, I say, let this rain ease off.

Robbie starts rolling a weed. I'm half pissed and me mind's gone. Robbie brings me back to reality with a jolt.

-Fuck me Rooftop, he says, are you doing that last fucker or not ?

-Yeah, I say, wait here.

I leave Robbie with the bags and the money and I carry Rory with me. I head for the front door of Marks.

I look round then head for the clothes section. Robbie's followed me in even though I told the cunt to stay outside. He's walking behind me trying not to look suspicious. There's more chance of him coming out of a British Rail refreshment bar looking refreshed than there is of him not looking suspicious. He's got one of them faces that looks out of place if it ain't in an Identity Parade.

I walk over to the coats. I'm puffing and blowing. There's some handy priced ones. I look at a couple priced forty eight quid. I think fuck it - grab one of these and flirt a quick cheque. I look in a mirror and notice me and Rory. He looks OK but I look like a bag of shite. I pick up one of the coats and we go into a changing cubicle.

I like the look of the coat, it's a sort of dark red thing. It looks OK - I wouldn't mind it meself. I try it on, but it's a piss poor fit. There's a little stool in the corner - Rory's balanced on it. He sees me staring and says,

-Yunka.

-No time for practising Esperanto now, I say.

I straighten meself up a bit, comb mine and Rory's hair. God, he looks like his fucking mother with his strawberry coloured hair. We both look the part. I take his dummy off him and put it in me pocket. He scowls.

-Never mind son, I say, you'll laugh about this one day - round about the time the Doctor gives out the medication in the Asylum.

I slip the coat back off and put me leather back on, and we're ready for business.

We walk out. I weigh up the assistants - not a lot to choose from. Two old girls, both grandmothers to look at them. I choose the one with least customers. She looks bored. As I get there she's serving a half caste lad. I stand back, clocking everything that's going on. He's paying by cheque. As usual me attention starts to wander. I should be concentrating but sometimes I'm about as focused as an Albanian non-export camera. I'm certain he's just passed her the cheque to run through a machine before she's took the card. Also I'm fairly certain it was blank. I'm thinking I must've seen wrong.

Anyway, she parcels up his gear and he fucks off. I plonk Rory down on the counter to the right of me. That way when I'm doing the cheque he'll be messing about, and if the signature ain't spot on she'll understand. After all, she's probably got grandkids herself. Rory looks at her and they smile at each other. Nice one kid, I'm thinking - you've earned your rusks today.

-Afternoon, I say, it's a little bit wicked out there.

Supergran smiles and says some pleasantry, but it's right over me head.

-Who do I make the cheque payable to? I say.

She smiles and says,

-Have you any other identification with you other than your cheque card?

Alarm bells start to ring in me head. Time to abort the mission. But she's smiling - it's probably company policy. I decide to buy meself some thinking time so I say,

-Yeah, I'll just nip back to me car and get me driving license.

Fuck this for a game of soldiers. I'm just about to pick Rory up and fuck off when she changes her mind and says,

-It doesn't matter, just pass me the card and a blank cheque please.

What the fuck's happening? What's the blank cheque shit? Something ain't fucking right. Scots John said something about Marks - what the fuck was it? I think calm down, look normal.

At this point everything is still in my possession. I've committed no crime. It might look unusual but I could just walk out of the shop. Fuck all could be said, I could even say,

-Oh, I need a shirt as well.

leave the coat on the counter and wait while she's busy serving someone else, and fuck off. I'm not thinking straight, the drink has clouded me head. I call Robbie for his weed but I'm fucking up good style cos of drink. Then I remember Big Tits in Chelsea Girl and I know this card ain't on any stolen list. Fuck the girl, she can have her blank cheque.

I pass her the card and cheque. Rory starts to try and get down off the counter. I'm pampering him, holding him steady but watching the old bird at the same time. Me heart's beating like fuck. I stare over at Robbie - he's watching every development. Me entire body is telling me that something is wrong. What the fuck did I give her that fucking card for? I had me chance, I should've fucked off.

She sort of puts the card through this machine next to the till. It gives her a read out. I can't see.

The smile fades on her faded fucking face. She runs it through a second time. What's it fucking told her? Panic time. Something major is wrong. She rings a bell under the counter, it goes off for maybe twenty seconds, but it lasts a fucking lifetime. The alarm bells are ringing for real.

I look around, I'm paralysed. Robbie's talking to me with his eyes. His eyes are screaming,

-Run, you fucking cunt....RUN !

The old girl has stepped back out of reach holding the card. She must think I'd slap her. God, I'd fucking like to. What do I do, what do I do, what do I fucking do?

I grab a hold of Rory and I run. I knock some man flying and I head for the stairs. I'm passing people, not stopping. I'm panicking. I'm in deep shit. I'm saying to people,

-My baby, my baby!

As I pass them.

I'm on the stairs - there seems to be more people coming up than going down. I can hear people coming the other way, about a flight down, and they're as anxious as me to pass people. I stop to a walk holding Rory close. I put his dummy in. Two Security Guards are on the way up. They pass me at the turn of the stair. Shits that pass in the night. I've stole the march on the fuckers - they've got to go up two flights and find out off Supergran what I look like - I'll be halfway through Salford by then.

I see the doors and I'm through them.

I'm on the street and I'm running. Rory's dummy falls out. There's no time to stop.

-Yunka, I say to him and he understands enough to keep his mouth shut.

RUNNING

I'm running for all I'm fucking worth. It's me and Rory against the world. So fuck you, world! I've got a good head start - I've got to keep the distance between me and the arseholes. Fucking Security Guards - three pound an hour wankers will have given up by now and rang the Dirty.

I'm flying when I hear a voice behind me,

-Stop him - Stop him...

What the fuck is this, *Bring Me The Head Of Alfredo Garcia*?

I don't look back, just keep moving. I'm skidding towards a corner. There's about six black lads stood at it. They block me way. For fuck's sake no! I can hear the voice again,

-Stop him - Stop him...

There's no way past. I look at the lads - they're all younger than me, but bigger and harder.

I plead with them,

-Don't do it, lads.

They say fuck all, they just sort of part and let me through. They ain't gonna let no fucker nail me. I shoot round a corner, then another corner. I'm a little way out of the Town Centre but not far enough. There's a pub at the bottom of the street. I head for it. I pass a bin and get rid of the cheque book. It's no fucking use to me now. It don't really matter if I'm caught with it or not. If I'm caught I'm nailed anyway, they've got a video in the shop, plus all the identification evidence. They'll remand me in custody till they find out where the book came from, and every place it's been Kited. Then they'll have at least twelve cases of fraud against me, not to mention theft and deception.

I slow down as I get to the pub door. As I go in there's some clown dressed as Superman coming out. He puts his tin under me nose and says,

-My name is Clark Kent, but you can call me Superman.

I put a load of shrapnel in his tin just to shut the cunt up and say,

-I'll expect a thank you letter from Haille Selassie.

It goes right over the Man of Steel's head.

I walk into the pub and sit Rory down, order a pint and notice the phone on the wall. I put me pint near Rory and go to make a call. There's a couple of taxi numbers next to it so I ring them both and order cabs right away. Out of respect for Superman, I order the cabs in the name of Mr Clark and Mr Kent.

Things are looking up - the taxi will be here in a minute. I sit down, take the top off me pint and check what's in me pocket. I've got four and a half quid left. I'll stay in the taxi till I've used three then jump a number eight into Salford bus station. I'll be home in time for tea.

I hope to Christ Robbie's had the sense to do one from Marks before the Dirty arrive. I don't want him arrested, he's got over three hundred quid and tomorrow's Swopsies on him.

I sit back, take a healthy gulp of me pint, and survey the wreckage of the day. Why do I fucking do it? Why am I a petty thief? I ain't stupid. I've always had jobs, some of them good ones. But I've never been able to resist a fucking earner. Even when I've known it's been suicidal to attempt something I've still had a go. The Kiting's a fucking classic. I knew from the beginning that it wasn't me game, but I couldn't leave it alone. You could call me a greedy bastard but that don't really explain it. I was in Skegness once; pocket full of money and I'm walking along the front with Margery, Brendan and Rory, and I just pick up a ball and keep walking. They were only about three quid. Where's the fucking sense?

I'm sat here mulling on this, waiting for either taxi and thinking it's been a twat of a day. Rory's his usual self, as good as gold. He's doing an impersonation of his mother and staring into space. I think that's it now with Kiting, I've had me Gypsy's Warning. I'll have a go at me big one - Cheltenham. I thought of it ages ago. What I'm gonna do is get a box number down there and open an account in an assumed name. Then get coloured brochures printed up, and from Christmas onwards run adverts in the *Sporting Life* advertising accommodation for the Cheltenham Horse Racing Festival. Thousands of Paddies travel over every year and every Guest House for miles around is booked to the gills. What I'll do is offer very reasonable digs at dirt cheap prices. Not too cheap to cause suspicion. Every cunt will get just what they want. I'll have fictitious accommodation, ranging from tenting facilities right up to cottages. I'll offer to cater for parties ranging from one man to a pub outing. I'll take an initial ten percent deposit with the remainder three weeks before racing. Then a few days before the off, I'll fuck off, dry up me Cheltenham accounts, then it's goodbye to Manchester for good. Margery will get a postcard from St Tropez. Imagine three thousand Paddies turning up to get their head down in the same cottage that ain't even being rented in the first place. It's a beautiful daydream, but I know in me heart I'll never fucking do it.

Oh well I'm thinking, when the pub door opens. I'm hoping it's the taxi, but it ain't - it's just Superman on a return visit to Metropolis. He looks round the pub, spots me sat in the corner, does an about face and fucks off out. The smoke alarm in me head goes off again. Some fucker's cooking meat, and I think it's me. Why'd the fucker be interested in me? I walk over to the window and find out why. It's *Gunsmoke* - the

Superhero's talking to two members of the Dirty and they're getting out of their van. Fuck me I think, just cos the cunt's dressed as an Intergalactic crime fighter don't mean he has to fucking do it. I mean, if the twat would've rented an Al Capone costume instead, would he have gunned down half of Farnworth? I look around - there's a back door. Fuck the taxis. I grab hold of the Boy Wonder and it's exit stage right.

We're in the pub's back yard. The gate's bolted but I undo it easy enough. There's a kid's bike on the floor, it's nearly new. I make a mental note to send Robbie back for the fucker and give it legs down the entry. It's full of dog shit and bins. I'm just reaching the end of it when I hear a voice behind shouting,

-Stop, Police!

I don't stop or look back. It's nothing personal; the only thing I've got against the Dirties is that they seem to be biased in favour of the innocent. I increase me pace. If this was fucking Manchester, it would take the cunts an hour to show up - these twats are here within fifteen fucking minutes and acting like Starsky and bleeding Hutch.

I turn a corner then another corner. I'm looking for a bus or a taxi any fucking thing that'll get me out of this cunt of a place. The Dirty are still behind me. I can't see them but I can fucking smell them. I pass this Volvo at a corner - he's waiting to pull out. I bang on the window. He winds it down. I say,

-Me kid's bad - can you run me to hospital?

I'm out of breath. He looks me over.

-Sorry, the bastard says, I'm in a hurry.

And he drives off. I hope that one day the cunt's genuinely in the position I was pretending to be in. I hope he's tear arsing down some fucking side street with his kid in his arms bleeding to death, and no fucker stops for him. I don't really hope that, I like kids; but fuck him anyway.

I look round; the Not-So-Serious Crimes Squad have turned the corner and are gaining on me. Twenty five years of running, and I'm still doing it now. If I didn't have to carry Rory I could out run these fuckers easy. There's three of them - the two Dirties and Superman, and they're all overweight. Superman's cape is flapping all over the place- faster than a speeding bullet, like fuck. In different circumstances I'd laugh me balls off. But I spit a mouthful of phlegm into the Bolton evening and take it on me toes.

I'm moving now for liberty's sake. I turn a corner and I'm in front of a Church. I put Rory on the wall, hop over and pull him after me. I'm in a graveyard. I duck past the stones. There's a big statue of an angel. Fuck me, I could do with a Guardian one at me side now. I'm knackered, me arms are aching to fuck but I've got to keep moving. I can't see the Dirty behind me, I think I've lost them. I come to the back wall of the cemetery. I get to it and there's a six foot drop on the other side. Fuck me, God, ain't you ever heard of an even bounce of the fucking ball? There's no way over with the baby. Just as I'm contemplating jumping - one small step for man, one giant step for mankind - a Dirty van pulls up on the road below. Fuck it, decision made for me - nothing to do but hide. I grab Rory and duck behind a gravestone. I pick a good spot - it's secluded, but it's still light. If it was dark nights, I'd have a fighting fucking chance. I put Rory down on me coat to stop him getting wet- he seems to be enjoying it. I hope he keeps quiet. I read the gravestone quietly:

-LEONARD ROLLINSON
BORN 12 APRIL 1907
DIED 10 APRIL 1957
LOVING HUSBAND OF ENID
REST IN PEACE

Fuck me, I think - poor cunt died two days short of his fiftieth birthday. You'd have thought the tosser would've hung on. Never mind, the family will have saved a few bob on presents and cards. I just hope they never planned no surprise party.

We settle down in the brambles and wait. It's funny, but for the first time in a long while, I think about Sellotape. Well son, if you could see me now you'd be pissing your sides.

Fuck them, fuck you.

ABEL MAGWITCH

It was the best of times, it was the worst of times. Like fuck it was. I'm done up like Abel fucking Magwitch in a fucking graveyard. With no hope of a fucking cruise to Australia as a bonus. I look through the stones - the Dirties have arrived at the gates. They're stood waiting there - fuck knows what for. Superman is next to them. They say something to him and he moves away. I think they've had enough of the have-a-go fucking hero; about fucking time. Some cunt must've told him I was Lex Luther. I crawl to the wall, SAS style, getting me trousers piss wet through for me trouble - the van's still parked below. It don't really matter; I couldn't jump anyway.

I wonder what all the fucking wait's about. Come on you bastards, you've got me cornered - don't make me suffer, put me out of me fucking misery. It's like when I was a kid and I did anything wrong - me Mam would put me to bed, and I'd have to wait till me Dad got home before I got hit. The fucking wait was worse than the fucking punishment. Every fucking footstep, every fucking noise, I thought was him. I'll tell you, it was a fucking relief when he finally got home and belted me.

Anyway, they give Superman the job of minding the gate. You'd have thought they'd have made better use of his X-ray vision. The two Dirties spread out - one takes the left side, the other takes the right. The fat Dirty takes the right, which is the side I'm in. I'll give the cunt his due - he's very methodical, and I'm thinking if he keeps this up I might get me wish for the cover of darkness.

I can hear his radio. It's all this Bravo Alpha Lima Lima Sierra balls. I'm praying there's a bank robbery round the corner and the pair of cunts are called away. But breaks like that only happen in fairy stories, and I ain't wearing no red shoes to click together. So I'm stuck where I fucking am.

Rory tries to get up, he's had enough.

-No soldier, I say, -stay put sweetheart.

He just sits back down again. God, the kid's good. I notice the laces on his trainers are undone so I tie them. I can't let the little swine get nicked improperly dressed.

The fat Dirty is going row to row and showing no respect for the poor sods under sod. I'm gonna have to make me move soon. If I sort of circle round him on me knees carrying Rory, I might just make it past him. But how the fuck do I get past Superman? I decide to sit tight and face the inevitable. I pick Rory up and dust him down. I wipe his nose and give him a cuddle. I'm a soft bastard, but I don't like the thought of the little twat getting his collar felt.

The fat bastard looks in my direction. I think the cunt's seen me. He seems to be missing graves out. He shouts over to the less fat Dirty,

-Trevor, over here!

The thinner fat Dirty comes over. They mutter together, fuck knows what about. One thing's for certain, they ain't planning a surprise party for Superman. They move away from each other. Trevor shouts,

-Whereabouts, Smithy?

Smithy points in my direction and says,

-Somewhere near the angel.

I think about a pub by the same name in Miles Platting, the one me and Margery sheltered from the rain in all those dreams ago and I wish I was there now. I sit the little fella on me knee - we're closer than Tony Curtis and Sidney Poitier in *The Defiant Ones*. I look at him, and think, I bet this kid never dedicates no rendition of *Pal of my Cradle Days* to his Dad. I lean back on poor old Rollinson's grave - at least I'm better off than him.

The fat Dirty moves towards me. I knew he'd seen

me now. There was no forward, only back. The only way out was past the fucker. I ain't gonna be arrested hiding behind no fucking gravestone. I'm gonna be on me feet like a man. What's that fucking saying? - 'Better to die on your feet than live on your knees'. I put Rory down and I stand up. I take hold of Rory's hand and I walk towards the Dirties. There's no way out. I'm fucking gutted. I was well and truly fucked. It was a definite prison sentence - two year fucking minimum. If they do their homework right on Kited cheques they'll be able to put two or three hundred on my toes. Fuck them. I was maybe twenty yards from the Dirty. Me head was spinning - they'd separate me and Rory, put him in a car, send for the Social Services, drive him to some fucking hostel before getting Margery out. The kid would fret - they've no right to fucking do that. Margery would explain what he was doing with me. We'd gone through what to say if the worst happened. She'd say we were separated, and that I called to collect him this morning and told her I was taking him to McDonalds. They'd put a supervision order on her. She'd have do-gooders on her back for a couple of year.

I'd do time. Big fucking deal; I've lived that shit before. We'd probably lose the house. I'd definitely lose me job - even them shitheads at the Council with their fucked up policies wouldn't wear this one. Margery might leave me, she might not - it's like the story me Dad told me about when he joined up to fight in the war. He said goodbye to his fiancee and she promised to wait forever. When he got back she was with another man.

-I wouldn't mind, he said, but I'd only got to the corner and realised I'd forgotten me 'bacca' tin.

The fat Dirty, Smithy, and the thinner one, Trevor, are joined by Superman. They're all stood still; they let me do the walking. They're all smiling. A good day's work for the fuckers, I suppose. Superman moves forward, that's all I fucking need. That would make the tabloids:

Caped Crusader Makes Citizens Arrest!

But they don't need Superman, I ain't gonna resist no fucker.

Me head's down and I feel sick. I look at Rory.

-Yunka, he says.

-Yunka, I reply.

We're both stood directly in front of the Dirties. The fat one's sweating and still out of breath.

-You're nicked son, he says, panting.

Fuck me, I think - a refugee from a Sixties TV cop show.

Superman walks up to the side of them. I look at the three of them and I try to think of something to say. But I'm lost in thought, as me life and criminal past flashes before me eyes. I see Sellotape dangling from a mill roof in the dark. I see Phipps's face when he can't find the punter's jacket. I see the Karaoke woman crying in the Angel. I see Jonesy's face when he got asked was he a Satanist? I see four empty chairs and Groucho in Blackpool. I see Lyons hurling his boots in the river. I see Kilkenny Benny having it away with five odd shoes from outside a shop on Oldham Street then selling them four pound a piece to a one legged man in the Pack Horse. I see the German, the Geordies, Scarlegs and a pair of lime green knickers. I see Bunny on a canal bank. I see Powell holding up a stolen watch. I see Vinny throwing the Two Hundred Club money out of a window in a sock. I see two mad Scotsmen on the Edinburgh train. I see me and Tony stood on a toilet seat avoiding Benediction. I see Margery seven month pregnant Kiting a Sony television. I see a fireplace in Miles Platting. I see me and Johnny Wright picking up a bed outside a furniture shop and walking off with it. I see Billy Kelly tear arsing across Piccadilly with a stolen suitcase. I see Jacko smiling and singing while waving a collection box. I see a girl in a pink smock pushing a blue cord pram. I'm stood in front of three clowns. The two Dirties and Superman. I remember what me Dad said about you're only beat when you admit you're beat. If you refuse to say you're beat, then you ain't fucking beat. It don't matter if you're bleeding from every orifice. It don't matter if they've got you pinned down, and laughing in your face. Just get as much blood as you can muster in your mouth and spit the fucking stuff right in their faces. I look at the faces in front of me, and I start laughing uncontrollably. They stand back like I'm off it. Then Superman takes a step forward.

-Watch it, I say, - I carry Kryptonite.

They move in. The thinner of the Dirties picks up Rory as the fatter one puts the cuffs on me. I look him in the eye, nod over at Rory and say,

-It was the midget that put me up to it.

And I laugh, and I laugh, and I fucking laugh.